PUFFI

Adèle Geras has had more than forty books published for children of all ages, as well as a poetry collection for adults. She is a voracious reader and loves the movies, the theatre, knitting, cats, good food and talking. She is also addicted to libraries, and visits her local branch on an almost daily basis.

Adèle Geras has lived in Manchester for the last twenty-eight years and is married with two daughters.

*Other books by Adèle Geras*

# THE FANTORA FAMILY FILES
# THE FANTORA FAMILY PHOTOGRAPHS

# A Lane to the
# Land of the Dead

### and other stories of the supernatural

## Adèle Geras

PUFFIN BOOKS

PUFFIN BOOKS

Published by the Penguin Group
Penguin Books Ltd, 27 Wrights Lane, London W8 5TZ, England
Penguin Books USA Inc., 375 Hudson Street, New York, New York 10014, USA
Penguin Books Australia Ltd, Ringwood, Victoria, Australia
Penguin Books Canada Ltd, 10 Alcorn Avenue, Toronto, Ontario, Canada M4V 3B2
Penguin Books (NZ) Ltd, 182–190 Wairau Road, Auckland 10, New Zealand

Penguin Books Ltd, Registered Offices: Harmondsworth, Middlesex, England

First published by Hamish Hamilton 1994
Published in Puffin Books 1996
1 3 5 7 9 10 8 6 4 2

Filmset in Bembo

Made and printed in England by Clays Ltd, St Ives plc

*For Ellie Powling*

## *Author's note*

The city in these stories is Manchester, and the places described are real, although I have changed some names here and there. All the rest is imaginary . . . as far as I know.

## Acknowledgements

*A Lane to the Land of the Dead*: the extract on page 5 from 'As I Walked Out One Evening', published in *Collected Poems* by W. H. Auden, edited by Edward Mendelson, is reproduced with kind permission of the publishers Faber and Faber Ltd.

*We'll Meet Again* . . . first appeared in *Beware, Beware* ed. Jean Richardson (Hamish Hamilton, 1987)

*The Centre* first appeared in *Knockout Short Stories* ed. Jane Joyner (Longman, 1988)

*Burning Memories* first appeared in *Mysterious Christmas Tales* (Scholastic, 1993)

*The Interview* first appeared in *Writing and Response* eds. Roy Blatchford and Jackie Head (Unwin Hyman, 1990)

*Miranda's Child* first appeared in a different version in *Woman's Own* (1986)

*Whispers from the Hotel California*: lyrics from 'Hotel California' are reproduced by kind permission of Warner Chappell Music Ltd and International Music Publications Ltd

# Contents

# A Lane *to the* Land *of the* Dead

*H*er. *I could choose anyone, but she's the one I want. Some of them are half dead before I reach them. Look at her, begging outside the Body Shop and still not afraid to look people in the eye. A bit of colour to her skin, too. Some blood still getting round there somehow. Yes. Her. She's the next.*

'Like a coffee, then?'

'Can't afford it,' Priss answered.

'My treat, of course,' said the young man. 'And a bun.'

She looked up at him, trying to appear surprised at the suggestion, shocked even. She wasn't a bit surprised really. She'd been catching sight of him for days, striding about the Arndale Centre as if he owned the place, all done up in black leather and silver studs, fancying himself rotten. He'd noticed her, too. She knew that. He seemed to keep walking past her. One day, he'd even thrown a couple of coins her way, and a lot of use they were. They looked foreign to Priss, although she couldn't make out the writing on them. I should have chucked them in the bin, she thought. I don't know why I kept them. The coins were in the back pocket of her jeans right this minute. Now he'd decided to talk to her.

She said, 'OK,' and stood up.

'Come on then,' said the young man, and began walking swiftly towards the Bus Station café. Priss almost had to run to catch up with him. I must be mad, she thought. He could be anyone. A murderer, a kidnapper . . . but he's offering coffee, and I can't stop thinking about that bun . . . maybe it'll have icing on it . . . or should I get a doughnut? All the way to the café Priss thought about food, dreamed about it. Normally, she tried to stop herself, tried to stop those daydreams because if you let them be, they filled your head up and food was all you thought about.

They sat down.

'I'll get you some stuff,' the young man said, and when he returned, Priss saw he had bought her a bun, a doughnut and a couple of KitKats, as well as a coffee.

'Those,' he said, pointing at the bright red wrappers, 'I'd keep for later.'

Priss blinked away tears. In the last six months, only Mickey and Skabber had been nice to her, and now here was . . . OK, Priss said to herself. Admit it now. He's gorgeous. You've been looking at him for days. You've been thinking about him a lot. Even back home at the Hovel-de-Luxe, you think about him when you're not figuring out ways to keep warm. And now he's buying you KitKats.

The young man sat and watched her silently as she ate her bun. She was just starting on the doughnut when he said, 'Homeless, then, are you?'

'No,' Priss said. 'I've got a room. It's OK.'

'Then why do you beg?'

'Extra money. Till I find a job. I'll find one now I've got an address. This is just for now.'

'Where's the room, then?'

'In Hulme. They're tearing down half the crescents.'

'A bit rough . . .'

'Yeah.' Priss ate her doughnut and thought of grey walkways, gaping windows, entrances piled with bags of rubbish, litter, stray dogs loping through the deserted streets, and the writing everywhere on the walls: *Love is not a crime.* She liked that. *Hulme for Hulme people.* She liked that too. She thought of St George's Church, derelict, but still beautiful; Zion Hall, kids still playing, still managing to look happy; brave little pubs still open in the wasteland all around them and said, 'Could be worse. They're building stuff too. There's something happening, anyway.'

'You run away from home, did you?'

Priss looked up. 'Do you have to wear those shades? I mean, we're inside, and it's Manchester out there anyway. In case you hadn't noticed, it's raining. It often does rain, up here. Are you from up here?'

3

'I'm not *from* anywhere,' said the young man. 'I just go about in the world, that's all.'

Oh, dead cool, Priss thought. That's a really informative answer. She sighed. She knew all about people who liked to pretend they came from California or somewhere. But he'd taken the shades off now.

'OK,' Priss said. 'I get the picture. Put them on again.'

'They're not that bad, are they? My eyes?'

'No, it's not that ... I just ...' She couldn't put into words why she needed those eyes to be covered. Perhaps it was the colour: a blue so pale that it was almost silver. Or maybe the fact that even a brief glance into their depths made Priss feel as though she were sliding down and down into water or ice ... it was better not to look. In order not to seem unfriendly, she added, 'Anyway, you haven't told me your name.'

'Angel.'

On anyone else, it would have been a silly name, but Priss didn't feel like laughing.

Angel said, 'Was it bad, at home? That why you left?'

Priss closed her eyes. It was none of his business. Suddenly she needed to talk to him, to tell him everything. She choked back the words. Never. She'd promised herself not to speak.

She said, 'You could say that. It's good of you to get me all this stuff, though. Ta.' She shifted in her seat. 'I ought to go now. I suppose I'll see you around.'

4

'You will. I'll come and see you in Hulme. I know it very well.'

'You don't know my address.'

Angel said, 'You'd be surprised. I know all the addresses I need to know.'

Priss smiled and stood up. Boys, she thought, they're all the same. Bullshit artists ... All the addresses I need to know, oh yeah! Some cool dude, or what?

'Tara,' she said.

He didn't answer. He just took off his sunglasses and stared at her and she moved out of the café, disconcerted by the spaces that opened out before her as she looked into his eyes.

Priss liked her room. Anyone else would have seen only the damp walls, the bits of glass missing from the windows, transparent curtains and non-existent carpets. She saw freedom, her own place, somewhere where she could simply *be*, without fear. People didn't realize, she thought, that Hell could have soft carpets and fitted cupboards and central heating. At school they'd read a poem and Priss wrote one verse down because it reminded her so much of her father's house. She knew it by heart and sometimes said it over to herself as she shivered under the thin blanket, to remind herself of what she had left behind.

> *The glacier knocks in the cupboard,*
> *The desert sighs in the bed,*
> *And the crack in the teacup opens*
> *A lane to the land of the dead.*

5

At first, the words had chilled her with their desolation, but now she found them oddly comforting: an incantation to keep her from harm; a lullaby.

*Her voice is like something I'd almost forgotten. Songs, or something. For a while, when she was talking to me, I didn't feel cold any more. Not quite so cold. I will find her. I will blow through the crescents and the walkways and over the scrubby grass and broken glass and bricks and find her, find her.*

Mickey was strumming his guitar and trying hard not to hear what Skabber was saying. The poor old bleeder only had two topics of conversation. Mickey thought of them as the two sides of an ancient, cracked 78 rpm record. Side B was The War, and this was definitely the A side. It was all about the Good Old Days, when slums really *were* slums, not like now when you could die at the side of the road for all the mind anybody paid you. We might've had no shoes (Skabber's speech went) and rickets and none of them mountain bikes or trainers or nowt, but by God, we had a Community! To hear him tell it, doors were never shut, neighbours were ready with nourishing soup at all hours and as for needles, guns, muggers, squatters and other kinds of general scum, there was none of that.

'And we had Unemployment,' Skabber would add. 'And a Depression. But were we depressed?'

'Not a bit of it,' said Mickey, right on cue. 'You put your best Vera Lynn record on and shined your shoes and went out to boogie at the Ritz.'

Skabber laughed, and Mickey went on, 'Anyway, I'm not a mugger. I'm a poet and I'm not unemployed, and even if I am a squatter, I keep the place nice, don't I? I don't see you complaining.'

'Poets don't work in Burger King,' Skabber said. 'Wouldn't catch Wordsworth working in Burger King.'

'I'm the Burger Bard,' said Mickey, who had dreams of being the next Bob Dylan. 'I like it. Gives me a bit of dosh, and then you meet people.'

'Her that's squatting in Ma Peters' old flat, you mean,' Skabber chuckled. 'That Priss. Nice lass.' He shook his head. 'What's she want to leave home for then, eh? Eh? Girl like her should be with her mum and dad.'

'She ran away from home,' said Mickey. 'She told me. She said she couldn't bear it any more.'

Skabber nodded and sniffed and began rooting in various hidden pockets for something to wipe his nose with. Mickey looked away while Skabber inspected a greyish rag-like thing he had just discovered, and tried to concentrate on thoughts of Priss.

He'd known as soon as he saw her, the day she first came in to Burger King, that this was it: Love. What those poets were all on about. He'd noticed everything about her instantly. He knew the chips she ordered were all she could afford. She knew he'd risked his job bringing her a burger some kid had returned because it had a gherkin in it. It was only after she'd been back a few times and they'd started chatting that Mickey had learned they were practically neighbours.

Destiny, he told himself. They were fated to be to-gether, Mickey knew. He was having a bit of trouble convincing her, but that was only natural. She didn't want to commit herself, she said. She was free. For the first time in her life, she could please herself, and she needed to be on her own after what she'd been through.

'What's that?' Mickey had asked her one night when they'd been standing on the bridge over the motorway, looking at a lemon-slice of moon and the moving headlights streaming like stars under their feet.

'I'm not telling,' Priss said. 'Not anyone. Not ever. That's over now. I've put it behind me.'

Mickey dared to say it then. The lemon-slice moon, the blue darkness, the cars humming below them went to his head and the cliché was past his lips before he could stop himself.

'I love you, Priss,' he said.

She chuckled and said, 'Give over, stupid,' but (Mickey consoled himself) she looked pleased. Anyway, that was what being a poet was all about, as far as he could see: suffering. Pining. It would give him something to write about when he'd got over the worst of the pain. Meanwhile he could feed her illegally when she came into the restaurant, and risk being sacked every time. He wouldn't have minded. It would have been a sacrifice, a measure of his devotion.

*She's never seen them, but I could show her. Cowering in*

8

*the corners of rooms with smashed-in windows, drifting along the grey balconies, crouching in doorways piled high with bin bags: they are everywhere. Their camouflage is admirable. Anyone who sees them thinks: druggie, Goth, hooligan, squatter, tearaway, punk, tramp, beggar . . . Oh, they can pass, all right, even the ones from long ago. There are enough strange creatures in strange clothes still around to give them cover, but I know them for what they are: the ragged, shadowy army of the Undead. Powerless. Disenfranchised. Indistinguishable from many of the living among whom they move.*

Priss walked along Market Street beside Angel, happily eating the chips he'd bought her.

'You don't come from Hulme, do you?' he asked.

'No. Lace curtains at the windows where I come from. Shaved lawns. Genteel.' She took another chip. Angel looked at her.

'So why did you leave?'

'I don't talk about it,' Priss said. 'I just wanted out, that's all. Everyone in my family . . . I can't explain. It all looked normal but it wasn't. No one spoke. There was coldness everywhere. Worse than coldness, really.'

'Cruelty,' Angel said.

Priss nodded.

'There's cruelty everywhere.'

'But it's not pretending,' Priss said, 'when it's here. Here you can see: houses boarded up, and there are tramps and drunks and all sorts, but you can *see* them. You can see the poverty and the crime and the badness . . . and anyway, they're starting to do something. Everything's being demolished, torn down. I like that. It means starting again. I believe in that. I believe you can start again. I'm going to. I'm not staying here forever.' She giggled. 'Sorry. You never asked for a soapbox speech, did you?'

'That's OK. You enjoy your chips. I'll see you again.'

He was gone before she could say goodbye, a black shape striding towards Cross Street, taller than anyone else, always visible.

*I can't. For the first time, I can't. She looks at me with a brightness I cannot bear. I will not touch her. I will not tell her how many of them are dead, those who come and go in the broken concrete. The dogs know. I can see them: Alsatians, bought to be a kind of burglar alarm, now abandoned, left to fend for themselves, racing through the ruins with a pack of thin, yapping mongrels behind them. Not hunting, but running away, as often as not, from the flapping sleeves of the Undead behind broken glass in darkened windows. I cannot, cannot think of her in that company.*

'Who was he?'

'Who d'you mean?' Priss answered, biting into her Giant Cheeseburger. It was Mickey's lunchtime and this cheeseburger was legitimately bought. Mickey finished his last chip.

'You know who I mean. Tall, white-faced bloke in black leather. I saw you in Market Street together. I nearly came after you.'

Priss took a sip of Coke. 'I can go for a walk, Mickey. You don't own me.'

'I know I don't. I never said I did. I only asked who he is.'

'He's called Angel.'

'Is he Spanish?'

'What do you mean?'

'It's a Spanish name. Lots of Spanish people are called that.'

'He doesn't sound Spanish,' Priss said. 'Anyway, I went for a walk with him, that's all.'

'Where do you know him from?'

'I just do. It's not your business. I have got a life, you know, apart from you. You're not my bloody father, you know.'

Mickey turned red, and then white. Priss groaned.

'I'm sorry, Mickey, I am honestly. I never meant to be horrible. I'm really fond of you. You know that. You *do* know that, don't you? I'd never want to hurt you.'

'No,' Mickey said. 'I know you wouldn't. It's OK.' He stood up. 'I'll see you tonight, right?'

'Could be,' said Priss. 'Ta for the burger.'


Priss sat on the bench outside the Body Shop and thought about Angel and Mickey. She tried to feel guilty about Mickey, who'd been kind to her. She tried to think about what he'd said, that time on the bridge. 'I love you, Priss.' She knew he really meant it. She knew he would look after her, so why? Why didn't she make things easy for herself by saying: yes,

11

OK. I love you too, and then they could be all lovey-dovey and devoted and together and take care of one another. She shook her head. The idea disgusted her. Love disgusted her. The kind of things people did to one another because of it disgusted her, and above all, happy-ever-after made her sick, because she knew that it was never like that. Not ever. She was a fool to have started thinking about Angel in the way she had. It wasn't a mistake she would ever make again.

He had come to her room last night. She'd seen him from the window and her heart rose up in her body and filled her throat as she looked at him, walking like a dancer along the pavement, scarcely touching it, almost floating. He came and stood under her window.

'Said I'd find you, didn't I?' he said.

Priss grinned. 'How did you do it? You're magic, you are.'

'Can I come up?'

'It's not very nice up here. Maybe I'll come down.'

'I have something to tell you.'

A chill went through Priss.

'Come on up, then,' she said, and stood trembling, waiting for Angel to climb the three flights up to her door. I don't care, she told a voice whispering in her head about danger. I don't care. I don't care.

They'd think I was a nutter, Skabber thought. Mickey'd say I'd been on the juice, and I haven't, not so bad anyone'd notice anyway. He'd say: Skabber, you're confused. That's what he always says. That or put a sock in it, Skabber. I wouldn't tell him. I wasn't going to tell anyone, but her . . . she's a nice lass, not like some around here. I should warn her. Tell her what she's dealing with. I've been in wars, I have, and I know what I'm talking about, I do. All that leather doesn't fool me, not for a second. I recognized him. I could smell him. I know who he is. He can't fool me. Not old Skabber, oh no. I know. I'll tell her next time. Next time I see her. It's not right. Not a nice lass like her.

Angel sat on a hard chair near the chest-of-drawers and Priss sat on the bed. He can't like me, she thought, or he would have come to sit next to me. He would have. He's almost as far away from me as he can get without being in a different room.

'Want a coffee?' she asked.

'I can't stay,' said Angel.

'I don't know why you bothered coming,' Priss said, suddenly furious, jumping up to stand by the window, blinking away tears. 'I never asked you. I never asked you for anything. You never had to buy me that coffee in the first place. Why did you?'

'I liked you,' Angel said softly.

'And now you've seen me a couple of times, and we've talked and you've decided you don't like me any more, is that it? Changed your mind? I'm not good enough for you.'

'No,' said Angel. 'I do like you. You're too good. I

like you too much. I've never . . . I have never felt this feeling before. It's new for me and I don't know what to do. I came to explain . . .'

'Are you trying to tell me you've never been with a girl before?'

'Thousands,' Angel said wearily. 'Millions, even. But you are different. I am feeling something different.'

This one, thought Priss, is worse than most. Thousands, indeed! Who needed him? Why did I let myself even think about him? It's my fault, she decided. I should have learned. If you make yourself soft, someone will tread on you, as if you were a slug. Oh, I haven't made myself stone yet, but I will. I will.

She said, 'I think you should go now. I want you to go and you want to, don't you?'

'I have to,' Angel said. 'For your sake.'

'Go on, then,' said Priss. 'Good riddance.'

'I can't even kiss you goodbye,' Angel said. 'I mustn't touch you.'

'I'd rather nibble a cockroach,' Priss said. 'I wish you'd leave. I wish I'd never met you.'

Angel stood up and went to stand next to her.

'Are you crying?' Priss laughed. 'Big macho type like you? Millions of women? What're you crying about me for?'

Angel said nothing. He opened the door and Priss listened to the sound his boots made on the concrete stairs.


Mickey and Skabber were sitting in the front garden,

14

which was what Mickey called the tiny patch of grass, just outside the squat.

'There's that fella I saw with Priss, look,' Mickey said. 'Told you about him, didn't I, Skabber? Didn't I tell you I saw her walking around with him the other day?'

Skabber nodded. There was something he should have told Priss, but he wasn't quite sure what it could have been . . . it was something to do with that man. Skabber peered at him now. He was tall, and wearing a leather jacket studded with silver. He was walking towards John Nash Crescent with his arm around Fat Myra, who lived out of two black dustbin bags in a pram, in one of the entrances of a block that'd been boarded up long ago. Fat Myra did cocaine. Fat Myra had done almost everything. She wore high, white stilettos and no stockings and a blue nylon lace dress under a man's army overcoat and no one knew how old she was. Skabber listened to her laughter, which carried clearly in the night air. He remembered now, remembered about the young man.

He said, 'Silly old cow, that Myra. Still, I wouldn't wish him on her.'

'Know him, do you, Skabber?'

'I've seen him. Here and there from time to time.'

'You're a liar, Skabber, that's what you are.' Mickey laughed. 'Reckon you know everyone, don't you? What's his name then, if you're so clever. Go on, what's his name?'

'Death.' Skabber cleared his throat and spat into the darkness, into the silence. Mickey said nothing for a few moments, then he giggled nervously.

'You're drunk again, you are. Shows how much you know. That's not his name. It's Angel.'

'Right,' said Skabber. 'Angel of Death.'

'You're nuts. Soft in the head. A whole packet of sandwiches short of a picnic, you are.'

Skabber sniffed. He wasn't in a hurry. They'd see. Oh yes. Tomorrow there'd be more coppers here than residents. Sometime tomorrow.

*It was easy. She was asking for it. She came up to me. Pressed herself against me and said, 'Oh, you're beautiful, so beautiful. Where have you been? I've been looking for you.' I could see that she had. Her face had lost its shape, as if the bones of her skull had melted. She'd recognized me instantly. There was a time when she thought I was a needle or a bottle or a knife in the twilight, but she was wrong, she said, and now here I was. Take me with you, she said. So I did. I took her somewhere hidden. The wall had been turned into a kind of lace, and boulders and bricks covered the ground, and there were bundles of rusty wires humming in the wind, singing. Kiss me, she said, oh, kiss me, and I did. My mouth was ice and she became still and heavy and I laid her on the bricks in the shadow of the grey lace of the wall, and there was no one who saw her last movements, no one to hear her last cries. After I had done with her, I felt nothing. She was my work. What I had to do. I don't care about this one. The one I care about I turned away from. This time.*

'Narrow shave,' said Skabber. 'That's what you had.'

'I don't know what you're talking about,' Priss said.

'Yes, you do. Don't want to admit it, that's all.'

Skabber poked something interesting from under one of his nails and examined it closely. 'I saw him. Tall, he was. Dressed in black leather. I saw him with Fat Myra. He had his arm around her.'

'It doesn't mean he killed her,' Priss said. 'Police said natural causes. Exposure, and stuff.'

'They don't know,' Skabber said. 'I know. I recognized him.'

'What's his name then?' Priss said. 'If you're so clever.'

'Mickey said, Angel. I said: right. Angel of Death.'

'God, Skabber, you don't half talk a load of cobblers,' Priss whispered, but she was trembling, remembering the eyes and the pale cheekbones and the thin fingers in which she could almost see the bones. He hadn't wanted to touch her. Was it because he knew that she would die if he did? Did he, could he, have loved her?

Sitting outside Humana, Priss looked for Angel, and sometimes thought she saw him: thin, tall, dressed in black leather. It always turned out to be someone else. I shouldn't look for him, she thought. Not now. She comforted herself that one day, somewhere, he would find her again.

# The Dracula Mask

On his way to meet Imran for coffee, Ray decided he loved Rusholme. I've lived here my whole life, he thought, and never really looked at it properly. All the spicy fragrance of restaurants like the Sangam and the Shere Khan and the Tabak tempted you in with promises of prawn bhutan and chicken tikka. The sweet centres displayed tidy trays of pink coconut squares, and honey-soaked baklava and delicious crumbly burfi. Where else, Ray thought, could you see so many different kinds of people, all shopping and eating and walking about together in one street? There were ladies in gold-embroidered saris, and punks and Sikhs; schoolchildren in uniform and old men in cloth caps lined up next to students in Doc Marten's outside the bakery, waiting for the day-old bread. And where could you find so many sorts of shop? The Kwiksave and the Ittefaq; the Chuni Saree House and the

Alankar Saree Palace; the Fancy Jewellers; the vegetable shops like Manchester Grocers and the Jilani Superstore, which laid their produce out on the pavement in boxes, so that you could see all the bargains as you walked by: nothing had changed since Imran's day, except that J F Blood and Sons had gone. Would he notice, after five years? When they were little, Ray and Imran had played pretend-games in which the shop played a part, just because of the name. Maybe Mr Blood was a zombie. Maybe a ghost. Or a vampire . . . maybe only vampires were allowed to shop there. They never went into the shop, but peered at it as they walked past on the way to school. It *looked* just like an ordinary junk shop, full of ordinary junk, but that was dull, so Imran and Ray made up stories about it. Or rather, Imran made up stories and Ray listened.

It was gone now. For ages after the shop closed, the name had still been there, but the whole of the front had had a metal shutter over it. It wasn't called J F Blood and Sons any more, and it sold a mixture of things like clothes-pegs and tea-towels and new Addis floormops and gifts, like swans with bathcubes piled up in between their wings.

Ray thought it was funny that after staying away from Rusholme for so long and going to another school, somewhere in Gatley or Cheadle, Imran should decide to come back to Xaverian College to do his A-levels. Imran was always clever, Ray thought, but he can't have such good memories of this place. That was why the family moved, after all. Or maybe it's me that's got it all wrong. Maybe they'd been intending to move all along, before everything. Before the Hallowe'en party was even mentioned. I haven't forgotten anything, Ray thought, going into the café and sitting down at a table by the window. He waved to Beanpole Brian, who was on duty, stringy and skinny behind the counter.

'Just waiting for a mate, Brian,' he said. 'That OK?'

'Fine,' said Beanpole Brian, busily arranging little wrapped bundles of biscuits in a straw basket.

Ray sat down facing the street so that he could see Imran before Imran saw him. It had been weird yesterday, bumping into him like that. Ray tried to work out the chances of a particular student at Xaverian meeting a particular trainee plumber in the street, and gave up at once. That was the kind of problem that made his head go all fuzzy and his eyes whizz round in their sockets. Imran could probably do it. Ray could still remember his first day at primary school, and how he had loved – yes, loved – the taller boy who had chosen him to play with. From then on, Ray had felt under Imran's protection. I would have done anything for him, Ray thought, and then laughed out loud, causing Beanpole Brian to give him a strange look from behind the silver curves of the coffee machine.

'It's OK,' Ray said. 'Something funny just came into my head.'

What a lie, he added to himself. Why did I say it was funny when it wasn't? Why did I laugh when I was thinking how what I did made Imran disappear

20

out of my life? I saved him. I saved him from something dreadful but that meant he had to go away, and
so I'd lost a friend. Only Imran and I know how
awful it could have been, and maybe he's forgotten.
Sometimes people forget things because to remember
would send them crazy. Maybe he's like that. Certainly he was friendly enough yesterday.

'Raymond!' he'd shouted, and run right across the
road and hugged Ray outside the DSS offices, in full
view of everyone. He'd got taller, of course, but
he was just the same: handsome and happy, with
his wide smile and his white, white teeth . . . Ray
shivered.

It had all started with Susie Makins' Hallowe'en
party. She'd begun talking about it as soon as they'd
gone back in September for their last year at primary
school. She may have mentioned it to some people
before the summer holidays, but the first Ray and
Imran knew about it was when Susie had come flirting
up to Imran, that day in the Boys' Playground and
said, 'It's my birthday on October thirty-first. You
know what day that is, don't you?'

'Hallowe'en,' Imran answered.

'I'm having a party. Can you come? It's fancy
dress.'

'Right,' said Imran. 'Great.' He tried to look as if
he didn't care much either about Hallowe'en or about
fancy dress parties, but Ray could tell he was excited.
Imran loved parties, and he loved dressing-up, because
he knew how good he looked as a warrior or a king
or even a humble peasant. The teachers always told

him so, over and over again, so Ray supposed it must have sunk in.

'See how Imran is doing it!' was the cry in every class performance since Infant School. 'Doesn't he look the part?'

More than parties and dressing-up, though, Imran loved anything spooky. He read every ghost story, horror story or creepy tale he could lay his hands on, and then he'd tell them all to Ray, either in the playground or as they walked home together through the twilight streets. He liked every possible kind of ghoul, ghost, spectre, or spirit, but best of all he liked a vampire, and of all the vampires in the world, Dracula himself was No 1. That was the way Imran put it: 'Dracula, Ray, he's the No 1. He's the best. The scariest of the lot.'

Thanks to Imran, there was soon very little about vampires that Ray didn't know. They had to be invited into your house. They were frightened of water. You couldn't see them reflected in a mirror. They were not fond of garlic or crosses or silver bullets, but the only sure way to kill one was to drive a wooden stake through its heart. During this vampire-craze, Ray and Imran used to peer hopefully into J F Blood and Sons, but it remained a junk shop and the man who looked after the shop remained perfectly normal.

'Maybe that's not J F Blood,' Imran said, 'the one who's in the shop, I mean. J F Blood probably doesn't dare to show his face. He's probably hidden away somewhere and only comes out at dead of night, after everything's closed.'

Imran lifted his arms high in the air, pretending they were batwings. But even after dark, nothing sinister ever really happened and Ray and Imran grew bored with their own imaginings.

As soon as Susie mentioned her party, though, Imran knew who he was going to be.

'It'll be easy,' he said. 'I've got a black suit. I got it for my sister's wedding. I'll ask my mother to make me a cloak, and I'll find some plastic fangs and go as Count Dracula. What about you?'

'I'll go as a scarecrow,' Ray said. He had the costume left over from another party.

'What's Hallowe'en-ish about scarecrows?' Imran said. 'They're not spooky.'

'Yes, they are,' said Ray. 'I think they are. They always look as if they've stopped moving just a second ago. They're creepy.'

'OK,' said Imran. 'I suppose so . . .'

Ray knew he'd lost interest in the whole topic of scarecrows and was busy imagining himself as Dracula.

The day before the party, Imran was still looking for a pair of fangs. Everyone in Rusholme had either never had them in stock, or else had sold out that very morning. Ray and Imran walked back from school, discussing the possibility of making fangs out of cardboard.

'They'd get soggy,' said Ray. Imran nodded sadly. 'Maybe we could buy some white plastic cups . . .' Imran's eyes widened.

'Brilliant! That's what we'll do. We'll cut fang shapes out of the plastic. They won't get soggy.'

'No,' said Ray. 'But you won't be able to eat or speak. Your fangs will fall out if you do.'

'I'll put them in my pocket while I eat. The rest of the time I'll just flit about silently. Dead spooky, I'll be.'

The boys were walking past J F Blood and Sons as Imran spoke. Ray glanced into the dusty shop window, as he always did, and he was the one to spot the mask. He stopped on the pavement, pulling at Imran's arm.

'Hey!' he said. 'Look at this! Isn't it fantastic?'

Imran looked. Right in the corner of the window, almost hidden by a tatty shawl and leaning against a brass jug was a mask: one of those luridly painted cardboard masks that fill newsagents' shops around the end of October. The kind that have elastic to hold them on to your head, and eyeholes so small you can hardly see out of them. This mask (which hadn't been in the window yesterday, Ray was sure of it) was like that but different.

'It's him!' Imran breathed. 'It's Dracula! I've never seen one of those. Those masks are usually witches and silly-looking monsters with lime green and orange paint all over them. This one's ace . . . I love that ghastly white.' His face fell. 'It'll be too expensive. What am I going to do?'

'I've got 85p,' said Ray. 'I can lend it to you, if you like.'

The boys went in. Five minutes later, they were on the pavement again, and Imran was holding the Dracula mask in a brown paper bag.

'Dead cheap, eh?' he said. 'I can't believe it. Brilliant!'

'That's 'cos it's second-hand. The man said.'

'I don't care,' Imran smiled. 'Look how good it is.' He took the mask out of the bag and held it up in front of his face. It seemed to be made from white, lifeless flesh. Ray knew if he touched it, it would feel like cardboard, but he didn't want to try. Imran's dark eyes glittered through the holes. There was a kind of gash where the mouth was . . . the fangs had been painted in, too, and small drops of blood dripped from them. Ray shivered.

'A bit too life-like, if you ask me,' he said.

'Death-like, you mean,' said Imran. 'Well, that's solved the fangs problem. I'm really chuffed.'

He giggled all the way home.

Ray looked up from his empty coffee cup. Beanpole Brian caught his eye.

'Bit late then, your friend, isn't he? Fancy another cup while you're waiting?'

'Ta, mate,' Ray said and went over to the counter to fetch it. 'You're right, though. He *is* always late. Can't think why anyone waits around for him, really.'

Back in his seat, Ray remembered the Hallowe'en party. Imran had even been late for that. There they'd all been, that Sunday evening, all the kids from Mr Henson's class, prancing around Mr and Mrs Makins' front room in old sheets with holes cut out of them for eyes, or pointy black hats, and black cloaks with tinfoil stars stapled on to them. Susie had put up Hallowe'en decorations, but the lights were on, and Mrs Makins was walking round with a big jug full of fruit cup, crying, 'Anyone want a refill?' It was exactly like every other party, and about as frightening as a game of Bingo at the seaside, until Imran arrived.

For ages, he simply stood at the open door until Mrs Makins lost patience with him and said, 'Oh, come in, Imran, for heaven's sake, you're letting all the heat out.'

Silence fell when he appeared. Ray stared at him and hardly recognized his friend behind the mask. Imran looked magnificent. The cloak falling from his shoulders was lined with satin as scarlet and liquid-seeming as blood, and it fell all the way to his feet. He appeared to have grown taller. He moved like a dancer. When he spoke, the voice from behind the mask sounded deeper, and as though it were coming from far away.

'Great costume, Imran,' Ray said.

'Imran?' said the voice behind the mask. 'I have never heard of this Imran. I am Blood. Jethro Blood.'

'J F Blood . . .' Ray laughed. 'That's good. You've come as J F Blood. What's the "F" for then?'

'Fear? Fangs? Fantasy?' said Imran. (Ray refused to think of him by any other name.) 'Take your pick.'

'How about "Friend"?' Ray said.

'"Friend" is good,' said Imran. 'Have you got a tasty neck for me to bite, Friend?'

'Give over,' said Susie, coming up to the boys at that moment. 'I know it's you, Imran. Have some cheese and pineapple toothpicks.'

26

Imran shook his head. Ray could see his eyes through the holes in the mask. They seemed to be looking at something very far away.

'There is nothing here,' he said suddenly. 'Nothing for me at all. I'm leaving.'

'But the party's hardly started,' Ray said. 'There's going to be a video later, Susie told me.'

'Videos!' Imran laughed. 'Paint instead of blood. Nothing real. Just flickering pictures, that's all.'

'Shall I come with you?' Ray asked.

'No, you stay,' Imran said. 'I'll see you at school tomorrow.'

Imran said goodbye and thank you to Mrs Makins at the door. Ray didn't hear what excuse he made. He was too busy looking at the mirror hanging on the wall behind Mrs Makins. There was her back reflected in it clearly enough, but nowhere in the glass was there any sign of Imran.

I've imagined it, Ray thought. I'm seeing things. I *did* have a bit of a headache before. Maybe I'm getting sick. He opened his eyes to look again, but by then Imran was gone and the door had slammed shut behind him.

During the next couple of days, Ray tried as hard as he could to remind himself that Imran was just Imran, his friend, and that the mask was nothing but a second-hand piece of junk, bought for a Hallowe'en party. The trouble was small things happened. They were not very important on their own, but in Ray's mind they added up. The main thing was Imran was looking ill. He was pale on the Monday, but by

Wednesday he had deep purple shadows under his red-rimmed eyes. His cheeks had sunk inwards, it seemed to Ray, and, maybe it was only imagination, but Imran's teeth appeared to have grown longer. Then there was that time in the cloakroom after school on Wednesday, when Robson had flicked some water from the tap at Imran, and Imran had shrunk in amongst the hanging blazers to avoid it. Later, Ray noticed that he kept rubbing at his hand.

'Have you hurt yourself?' he asked Imran on the way home.

'It's nothing,' Imran said, but Ray could see the blister on the back of Imran's hand, just as if he had been burned. He said nothing, but thought of the Dracula mask. It seemed to him that the mask was what was causing the damage. Ray thought, I'd like to get rid of it, but how? And would Imran ever talk to me again if I did? How would I get hold of it? Where does he keep it?

He said, 'You know the mask . . . where do you keep it?'

'It's in my schoolbag. I take it everywhere.'

'But you can't wear it at school. Why do you bring it?'

'I don't . . .' Imran hesitated. 'I don't like to be too far away from it.'

'Why?'

'It gives me power.'

'What power?'

Imran looked at Ray. His eyes, the old Imran's bright, lively, smile-filled eyes were flat and lifeless as dark pebbles.

Ray shuddered and said, 'No, don't tell me. I don't want to know.'

That night he couldn't sleep. What were you supposed to do when your best friend started to turn into a vampire? The only thing he could think of was the mask. If only that could be destroyed, then Imran would be safe. The power, whatever it was, would leave him. The problem was going to be stealing the mask from Imran's bag. How could he possibly do that without anyone seeing him? Towards morning, Ray fell asleep, and dreamed of Imran flying over Rusholme with his scarlet cloak streaming out behind him.

If it hadn't been for the fight at breaktime, Ray could never have done it. Someone said something. Thicko Robson, of course. He called Imran a name. Paki. Something like that. There was always someone like Robson, in every class, jealous of Imran, full of hate and anger and ready to use his fists. The old Imran had had the odd scuffle, but now . . . everyone fell back as Robson was pinned to the ground. Imran seemed almost to fly across the space between them, and he left his schoolbag lying by the wall.

The fight could look after itself. Ray had only one thought in his head. Find the mask and get rid of it. At once. Dimly, as he scrabbled about in Imran's bag, he was aware of voices.

'Sir, sir, it's Imran . . . he's biting, sir . . . Robbo's hurt, sir . . . blood, sir, there's blood . . .'

Ray had found the mask. He stuffed it down the front of his anorak and ran out of the school gates. The mask, lying over his heart as he ran, felt clammy, cold. Ray didn't know where he was going. His only thought was to put as much distance between himself and school as he possibly could. In a street he didn't know very well, he stopped running and got his breath back. Nobody had cleaned up the rubbish from round here for ages. Ray took the mask out of his anorak and held it away from him with the tips of his fingers, as if it were a dead thing, something rotten. What, he thought, am I going to do with it? At first he considered putting it into one of the overflowing wheelie bins that lined the street, but he knew that wouldn't be good enough ... this mask needed something more. Ray stepped aside to avoid a deep puddle, and then it came to him. Water. He would drown the mask in the puddle and see what happened. If only he had a wooden stake ... but would a stake be any use without a heart to drive it through? Perhaps a piece of wood through the eyes would do? Ray looked around for something wooden. All he could find was a couple of ancient ice-lolly sticks. He picked them up and pushed them into the cardboard right next to the eyeholes of the mask. Then he laid the mask in the puddle, with the lolly-sticks poking up, looking silly. I hope no one is watching me, he thought. They'll think I'm mad. The street was deserted, which was lucky. The mask had begun to curl up at the edges, to dissolve as though the puddle it lay in were some kind of acid ... a smell

rose from it . . . the gash of the mouth had widened.
It was twisted now, gaping, wrinkling. The cheeks
were crinkling up and up, like a sheet of paper in a
fire, and soon there was nothing left of the mask at
all, except the elastic that held it on to a human head.
The lolly sticks floated on the black water of the
puddle, and there was a greenish scum all around
them.

Ray ran all the way back to school. Break had
ended ten minutes ago, but no one was bothered.
Everyone was still talking about the fight. Robbo had
gone off in an amulance. Imran had been taken home
in the Head's own car.

'He looked awful,' Susie Makins said.

'Robbo looked worse, though,' said Mick Thomas.

'There was blood everywhere,' Nora Philips added,
but it was what Titch Hutchinson said that made Ray
sick. He didn't say it to everyone. Titch never did talk
to many people, but he said it to Ray, because he
knew Imran was Ray's special friend.

'There was blood all round Imran's mouth,' said
Titch. 'His teeth were all red.'

Ray looked down at the dregs of his second cup of
coffee. Where *was* Imran? Would he chicken out?
Not turn up at all? He'd disappeared quickly enough
after the fight all those years ago. For three days, Ray
hadn't dared call round and confess to what he had
done with the mask. By the time he'd plucked up
courage, Imran had been moved to his big brother's
house in Leeds, and there was a 'For Sale' sign outside

31

the house. The next thing anyone knew, the whole family had moved. Ray had waited and waited for a letter. Or a phone call. Imran knew his number well enough, but there had been nothing but silence. And now Imran had turned up again, at Xaverian.

'Ray!' said a voice. 'Hey, man, dead sorry I'm late.'

'It's OK, Imran,' said Ray. 'Sit down and I'll get you a coffee.'

Imran sat. Ray came back with the coffee. Then the talk began. Ordinary things. A-level subjects . . . how's your mum . . . seen any of the old crowd . . . what are you up to . . . plumbing, that's nice . . . whatever became of . . .

Then Ray said, 'Remember that shop? J F Blood and Sons? Where you bought that mask? It's gone now.'

'Yeah, I did notice. Shame really.' (Dead cool, dead nonchalant, as if he didn't remember the mask at all.)

'Do you know,' said Ray, 'what happened to the mask?'

Imran said, 'How do you expect me to remember a thing like that after all this time? I expect I lost it. It was only a tatty second-hand bit of cardboard, after all.'

'You didn't lose it,' Ray whispered. 'I destroyed it. I had to. It was destroying you.'

Imran laughed. He opened his wide, wide mouth and showed all his very white teeth.

'Pull the other one,' he said. 'It's got bells on it.'

Ray thought of telling him: the puddle, the lolly sticks, everything, and then thought better of it. Imran had clearly forgotten. Either because he needed to forget or because Ray had genuinely saved him, and the memory of those awful days had faded and faded until it had gone completely. Ray wanted to say: if it weren't for me, mate, you'd be a vampire. How about that? Instead, he said nothing, and listened to Imran describing all the groovy people who were in his class at college.

# The Phantom *of the* Library

I don't normally work for my GCSEs in Didsbury Library. Some of my teachers would say I don't normally work, but that's not true. If I'm interested in something, I don't mind trying really hard at it. Usually I do all the trying in my bedroom, but this time I had to clear out and go to the library because my room was being painted, and if I worked in the kitchen or dining-room, my sister, Prue, who is only six, would want to play and scribble on my stuff, and my grandma, who is old and chatty, would want to come and have a natter.

If she saw it was a History project I was working on, she'd say, 'History! I could tell you some of that. I go back ever such a long way.'

'Not as far back as Ancient Egypt, though,' I'd say, and she'd chortle. It had become quite a comic routine.

So there I was in the library. I practically live in the library. I know all the regulars. I borrow books and return them. I read magazines and look at the CDs, but I've never done homework there before. It was the Tuesday morning of the October half-term. For once, it was quiet in the Reference Section. The whiskery character who fluttered newspapers in a special way that made them crackle hadn't turned up yet, nor had the person in the blue anorak who kept looking through the London telephone directories. There was just me, and in front of me a high pile of shiny books I'd hunted out. I was thinking about Pharaohs and mummies and pyramids and was even considering writing some of my thoughts down when I heard a noisy munching, coming from the table behind me. I froze. I'd been coming to this library all my life and I knew that one thing that sent Miss Thomson mad was people eating. She was as kind as could be at all other times, ready to do cutting and sticking and stories with the little ones, willing to trail round the shelves in search of fat books with pictures of red-headed women in shawls and clogs for her oldest readers, and happy to hunt out anything she could on Ancient Egypt for me. But an eater – the minute she saw even the corner of a crisps packet poking out of a schoolbag, she turned into a dragon.

'I hope,' she would say, 'you are not intending to eat those in here.'

'Oh no,' the person would assure her, feeling smaller by the second.

'Good,' Miss Thomson would say. 'There are several perfectly good benches, just outside.'

So I was shocked by the sound of open apple-munching. This had to be someone who had never been in the library before. All Miss Thomson's regulars knew what was what. I had to warn this poor new kid of what was in store. I turned round to say something and said nothing for a full minute.

In the end I muttered, 'Who are you?'

'I,' said the person sitting at the next table, 'am Sir Edmund Hugh Alexander Fairfax de Vere Cavendish. And what would your name be, my young friend?'

'Guy Matthews,' I whispered. 'You can call me Guy.'

'And you may call me Sir Edmund.' He took another bite of his apple and I had time to get a good look at him.

'Are you an actor?' I asked. 'Why are you all dressed up like a cavalier? Is it for TV? Are they filming in Didsbury?'

Sir Edmund looked down at his brocade sleeve with a broad lace cuff, his handsome leather boots, and the wide-brimmed hat lying on top of last week's *Times Educational Supplement*. He smiled.

'I am dressed like a cavalier,' he explained, 'for that is indeed what I am. I am exceedingly gratified that you are able to see me.'

'Of course I can see you,' I said. 'You're sitting there eating an apple and if Miss Thomson catches you, she'll have your guts for garters.'

Sir Edmund let out a bellow of laughter that made me wince. At this rate, he'd get thrown out for noise before Miss Thomson ever twigged about the apple.

'Guts for garters! How droll! How fanciful a conceit!'

I decided that this man was a serious nutter. I looked at him carefully, thinking that the police would probably need to know about him eventually. He was about forty, with a reddish face, and a brown moustache. He had a little pointed beard stuck on the end of his chin. His hair hung almost to his shoulders. He was extremely solid and visible.

I said, 'Why did you say you were glad I could see you?' What was this man trying to tell me?

'Because, my fair young scoundrel, I have been trying to manifest myself for nigh on three hundred and fifty years and have only today, it seems, succeeded.'

'Manifest yourself?'

'The spectral life is harder than you may imagine. It takes years of trying – centuries in my case – to (how should I express it?) solidify sufficiently for anyone to see you. Or hear you if it comes to that. It requires not only a supreme effort on the part of the phantom involved but also the happy conjoining of what has to be seen with a receptive person who can see it. In other words, boy, I owe my visibility to you, and I am indeed more grateful than you may imagine, as I shall shortly explain.'

'Hang on a mo,' I said, stopping him. I gulped. Wasn't I supposed to be terrified? Shouldn't I be gibbering with fear? Well, I wasn't. Sir Edmund was not a bit threatening. Still, ghost or no ghost, I could see he was one of those people who, if you let them, will keep talking for ever. 'If you're a ghost, then

37

how can you eat a real apple and make real apple-munching noises?'

'The apple,' said Sir Edmund, 'is no more real than I am. Purely an illusion, I do assure you.'

'How long have you been haunting Didsbury Library?' I asked.

'It has not been a library for very long, you know. I can remember what it looked like when we camped here with Prince Rupert's army, before the Battle of Marston Moor. Nothing but fields and trees then, of course. And tents, and horses and so forth, naturally. Still, those who built this library excelled themselves. Do you not admire the battlements? The flying buttresses? The mullioned windows? The carved stone rosettes? Very suitable for someone like me. I have been thoroughly at home here. The staff are friendly and kind, but alas, in spite of my best efforts, not one of them has ever seen me. Indeed, I may go so far as to say that you are the only living creature in the last three hundred and fifty years to have caught sight of me. You are especially privileged. I can see, moreover, that you are suited to the task I have in mind for you to perform.'

'Task?' I went pale. I didn't much like tasks in general, and I didn't think I liked ghostly tasks in particular.

'A trifling thing for one such as yourself,' said Sir Edmund. 'I wish you to tell the world of my existence. I wish you to provide me with Publicity!'

'Publicity?'

'Precisely. I have learned about Publicity in the last

few years. I have been floating about here for a very long time. I did not manage to manifest myself in time for my Centenary, nor for my bi-Centenary, nor for my Tercentenary. This year, however, 1994, is my Tercentenary-and-a-half and I should like to mark the occasion in some way.'

'What way?'

'Oh, nothing too extreme . . . the odd T-shirt. A commemorative mug, perhaps. Postcards? Souvenir key-rings? Possibly crystal paperweights? Every common or garden headless horseman or murdered serving-wench has a story. The Heritage Industry, as I believe it's called, thrives on tales of far lesser spirits than myself. I, after all, am a de Vere Cavendish!'

'Were you horribly murdered? Are you seeking revenge?'

Sir Edmund shook his head. 'I died of a fever. It was very damp, camping at Barloe Moor. It still is rather on the damp side hereabouts, I find.'

'That's it, then. That's why you've had no publicity. You aren't frightening enough.'

'Not frightening enough.' Sir Edmund considered this for a moment. 'Oh dear. Still,' he looked a little more cheerfully at me and winked, 'I have been up to all sorts of mischief. Oh, yes, mischief and mayhem.'

'Like what, for instance?'

He had to think a bit about this.

'I change the books around frequently. I mislay the covers of CDs. I cross things out on lists just to cause confusion. I hide the Review sections of the newspaper simply to irritate readers. I steal this and that from the

39

wine-merchant and the excellent fruiterer on the corner who displays his wares outside the shop . . .'

'I thought you said the apple wasn't real,' I said.

'Do not interrupt, sirrah! I never said I ate what I stole . . . oh no. I redistribute things . . . all sorts of passers-by have suddenly found they are in possession of some tasty morsel or another . . . where was I? Ah, yes . . .' He leaned towards me. 'A short while ago, I did a most fearsome and terrible thing.'

'What?' I asked, imagining librarians buried alive in underground vaults. 'What did you do that was so awful?'

'I stole the gargoyles!' he hissed. 'Wrapped them in a bin-bag and threw them into the back of a rubbish-truck.'

'That's horrible,' I said. 'I liked the gargoyles. Everybody's missing them. They're busy collecting money to replace them. I think that's a mean trick.'

'You have to understand my plight, young man. Would you care to be ignored for three and a half centuries? Furthermore, perhaps it was that wickedness itself that has, as it were, made me into a bona fide visible phantom. Perhaps the worse you are the more people see you. Have you thought of that?'

'Well, I can see you,' I said, 'so you can stop mucking about with our library.'

'I will,' said Sir Edmund, 'if you will publicize me.'

'How?'

'You mentioned television? Or perhaps the newspapers. Print is the more substantial medium. The one I am used to. Television seems sometimes as spectral as

40

I am!' He laughed his enormous laugh again. 'Will you help me?'

What could I say? I nodded.

'But first,' I added, 'we'll need to find out if anyone else but me can see you.'

No one else could. Over the next few days I did several experiments with all kinds of different people, but not one of them could either see or hear poor Sir Edmund.

I actually told Miss Thomson about him. I explained about his tricks. I even told the story of the gargoyles, and all she said was, 'Guy, dear, you've always been one of our best readers, ever since you were a tot, but there *is* such a thing as too vivid an imagination, you know!'

By the end of the week, poor Sir Edmund was feeling quite gloomy. I went in to chat to him every day except Wednesday, when the library is closed. Even on Wednesday I saw him when I went shopping with my mother and sister. He was striding backwards and forwards on the little battlement over the library porch, and when he saw me he took off his hat and waved it at me and I waved back.

'What are you waving at nothing for?' Prue asked.

I didn't bother to answer her, but I was becoming more and more depressed.

Then I had an idea.

'I'll take a photograph of you,' I told Sir Edmund. 'I'll borrow my mum's Polaroid and we can see how it comes out straight away.'

I didn't tell him that in photos, ghosts generally came out like a sort of blur. I thought it was worth trying and Sir Edmund was tickled pink. He posed like a Supermodel outside on the benches, up on the battlement, sitting at a table in the Reference Section. I used up half a film, because the results were better than my wildest dreams.

'I'll take them straight round to the *South Manchester Reporter*,' I said. 'They'll believe me when they see these.'

Sir Edmund had never seen himself in a photograph before.

'Wondrous!' he kept saying as we watched the pictures developing. 'Most fantastical and wondrous!'

'You wait here,' I told him. 'I'll be back in a minute.'

*The Reporter*'s office was just around the corner, down School Lane. I shoved the photos into my anorak pocket and ran all the way there. I arrived at the counter panting and red-faced.

'Yes, dear,' said a lady. 'Can I help you?'

'I must see the Editor at once,' I said. 'I've just taken some photos of a real-live ghost.' I giggled. 'Well, a real-dead ghost, if you get what I mean.'

'Just a minute, dear,' she said, looking nervous now, as though I were a dangerous criminal.

A man in a suit came out of the office to talk to me.

'Photos of a ghost, then, sonny, is it?' he said. He was smiling in a smirky sort of way that showed he didn't believe me. I *hate* being called 'sonny' as well. I'd soon show him.

'Yes,' I said. 'Photos of Sir Edmund de Vere Cavendish, who has been haunting the site of Didsbury Library for three hundred and fifty years. Did you know Prince Rupert's army set up camp there before the Battle of Marston Moor?'

'Yes,' he said. 'Everyone knows that. There's a blue plaque on the wall of the library that says so.'

'I've got photos of him,' I said. 'Here.' I took the snaps out and laid them on the counter, without even looking at them.

'Sir Edmund de Vere Cavendish, you say?' he muttered.

''Sright.'

'Where exactly?'

'There.' I pointed at a photo.

'That's you,' he said kindly, 'and some kind of fault on the film as far as I can see.'

He was right. Poor Sir Edmund had faded. In the few minutes since the photograph had been taken, his image had drained right out of the paper and all that was left was a whitish fuzziness. I mumbled some kind of apology and ran out of the door. I wouldn't be going back to *The Reporter* offices in a hurry. On my way back to the library, I thought of what I would tell Sir Edmund. He would be so disappointed. It was as I passed the TV and radio shop on the corner that I had my second idea. I would record his voice: interview him. Get him to tell the story of his life as a ghost, in his own words. That would cheer him up. He would have to come to my house to do the recording, but I didn't think he'd mind that. He must surely be eager to see some new places after hanging out at the library site for years and years.

Sir Edmund throughly enjoyed his recording session. He made me play the whole interview back to him three times. The Fast Forward button intrigued him. By the time he left to float back to the library, he was happier than I had ever seen him. But I did notice that he was becoming a little less solid. Sometimes lately, when we'd been chatting, I'd noticed that I could read the titles of the books through his body. Now that I had him on tape, though, I felt better. He could fade away peacefully and not be forced to wander around seeking publicity for the next however many years. I would take the tape myself to the BBC building, and hand it in to Greater Manchester Radio. I would tell them all about Sir Edmund. He'd be listened to by millions. Just to make sure the sounds weren't only in my head, I called Prue in.

'Listen to this, Prue,' I said. 'Who's this talking?'

She listened carefully while I played her a few minutes of the tape.

'It's you,' she said, 'talking to a man who sounds very far away.'

'But you can hear him? You can hear what he's saying?'

'Yes, but it's getting quieter and quieter, isn't it?'

I let the tape run to the end of the interview. Prue was right. Sir Edmund's voice was disappearing as surely as his face had vanished from the photographs. I knew, I just knew that the next time it was played, there would be nothing there at all. What was I going to tell him? I was up half the night worrying about it.

The next day, I couldn't find Sir Edmund anywhere. I sat in the corner of the children's library, which was the only place I could find that had no one else in it.

'Where are you?' I whispered.

'Right beside you,' said Sir Edmund, but the voice was thin now. I could hardly hear him.

'I can't see you,' I cried. 'And I can hardly hear a word you're saying. Sir Edmund, come back ... please.'

'Such an effort ...' said a breath near my ear. 'So much hard work, dear boy.'

'But the publicity! What about that? What about the Tercentenary-and-a-half this year? Telling everyone about you? Speak to me, Sir Edmund. Don't go away!'

'Write ...' said a voice. 'Write my story. I will always be here. Tell them.'

I have written this story now, all about my friend the cavalier. His name is Sir Edmund Hugh Alexander Fairfax de Vere Cavendish, and he is there in Didsbury Library, even if you can neither see nor hear him. This year, 1994, is his Tercentenary-and-a-half. Please remember him and all other ghosts who find Publicity a problem.

# We'll Meet Again...

'Fan-tastic!' Maddy said, as she peered short-sightedly into a mirror that was, as she put it, 'more spots than silver'. She was wearing a brown felt hat and a brown woollen coat, with a fitted waist and a skirt that nearly touched the ground. 'This'll be more your size, Celia. You'd better try it on.' She took the coat off. 'Wherever did you get all this stuff? It's really amazing. I mean, it looks authentic.'

'It is authentic.' Celia was pulling the brown coat on. 'Honestly, Maddy, can't you do something about the mirrors? It's difficult to see what you look like . . . what kind of shop is this, anyway?'

'It's not a shop. Hadn't you noticed? Just an over-sized box full of second-hand clothes. My customers are used to it. If they want mirrors, they can go to Jaeger or Next or somewhere. Cheapo style, that's what I'm about. These are great, honestly. Forties is all the rage. You said they were authentic. Where did you find them?'

'I was given them. A man in our street let me take them. He was clearing up after his wife died.' Celia paused. 'She died about two years ago, actually. I think he couldn't bring himself to clear up her stuff, and get rid of it . . . not for ages . . . anyway, when I got there, it was all ready in that box.'

'Dead sad, really,' said Maddy, 'when you think of it. Did you know her? The wife?'

'Well,' said Celia, 'by sight, you know. Not to talk to, not properly. My mum used to go in there and have a chat now and then. She was fat . . . not very pretty. Not when I knew her . . .'

Maddy had stopped listening and gone to lure a couple of helpless-looking people into her clothes-box. Celia stood in front of the mirror and tried to see herself in what little light there was. I look good, she thought. It suits me. Mrs Stockton was skinny like me, back in the Forties. He said so. I wonder how much Maddy'll want for it.

Mr Stockton had been standing by the sideboard when she went in. 'Just a few things belonging to Irene,' he said, and twisted his head round as if he didn't want to look at anything, not at her and not at the clothes. 'They're no good to me now.' That's what he'd said, and then he'd laughed. 'Not much good to Irene either for a long time. She got too big for them in the end. There was a time,' he'd rubbed a clenched fist along the edge of his chin, 'when I could have put both my hands in a circle round her waist.

47

She wasn't any thicker than you are now, a slip of a thing, was my Irene . . .' His throat had filled up then, like someone with a chesty cough. She thought he was having a hard job keeping himself from bursting into tears.

She'd said quickly, 'My friend Maddy'll like these. She's got a kind of stall in Affleck's Palace.' He didn't know about the Palace. She'd told him, 'It's where you go in Manchester for good, exciting, second-hand stuff. Is it all right? Taking it there?'

He nodded then. 'Yes, Irene was fond of young people . . . would like to think of them enjoying her clothes. You should try some,' he'd said, 'you're the right size . . .'

'Oh, I couldn't,' she'd said, and now here she was in Irene's coat, and he was right. It was beautiful. Anyway, then she couldn't think of anything else to say, so she'd picked up the box. Looking back, she could see him standing in the window, stroking the back of his hand along his jawline.

'That looks great,' said Maddy, when the customers had gone. 'You should keep it.'

'How much do you want for it?'

'I'll let you have it for nothing. A kind of commission for bringing this treasure to me, and not trying to flog it to anyone else. You can have a dress too. There's got to be something . . .' She started rummaging about in the cardboard box. 'Here you go.' She held out a soft, slippery bit of what looked like nothing very much. 'Try that on.'

Celia went into the small space behind the bit-of-fabric-on-a-string that served Maddy as a fitting room. This isn't like me, she thought. These aren't my type of clothes at all.

Almost as though she had overheard Celia's thoughts, Maddy spoke from behind the curtain.

'I know it's not your type of gear, Celia, not really, but you should think about it seriously. I mean, that Forties look really does something for you. You can wear that dress to the Forties Night next month.'

'What Forties Night?' Celia said, pulling the curtain back.

'Wowee!' Maddy shrieked. 'You look like a film star from one of those old black and white thingies . . . What do you mean, what Forties Night? Every few months they have one . . . down at the Ritz. Everyone dresses up and the music is Glenn Miller and stuff like that. It's great . . . you must come, Celia. Promise you'll come.'

'Not got anyone to come with, have I?' Celia said, pulling the curtain across again. 'Still, I like the dress. I'll have that, and thanks a lot.'

'Don't mention it,' said Maddy. 'And you don't need to have a partner. You can come with me and Graham.'

Celia muttered something about gooseberries as the dress came up over her head.

'You'll meet someone there,' Maddy said. 'Do say you'll come. Go on . . . you've got such a perfect outfit, that dress in this wonderful slippery material with those lovely blue leafy patterns all over it . . . and the coat on top of course. Please, Celia.'

'Right,' said Celia. 'I'll come. I'll probably regret it, but I'll come.'

'Terrific,' said Maddy. 'Just for that, I'll let you take your things home in a carrier bag. Aren't you lucky?'

Later that same day, Celia struggled up the sloping pavement to the station, wishing the books she had to carry to college were lighter, wishing that Maddy's carrier bag had a decent handle, one that didn't cut your fingers as you held it. She was wearing the brown woollen coat and had put her anorak into the bag, but it didn't make it much lighter. She stood on the platform waiting for the train to Birchwood, watching the dusk wrap itself, mauve and grey and pink, around buildings which suddenly looked soft at the edges. Only October, she thought, and the evenings are coming earlier and earlier.

When the train pulled in, she opened one of the doors and then stood aside to let a weary-looking woman hung about with a folding pushchair, crying baby and assorted bits of shopping, get on before her. Celia slammed the door shut and looked out of the window as the train slowly slid away from the station. Someone was standing on the platform, waiting, looking up and down the line, as if expecting to see someone ... Celia, who wasn't looking carefully, caught only a glimpse, and by the time she looked back, the figure had shrunk to almost nothing, but it seemed to her that the woman was wearing a brown coat very like hers. She was still peering up and down the platform, up and down . . . Oh well, Celia said to herself, Maddy said Forties styles were in. They must be more in than she thought. I'd better find somewhere to sit.

She sat down in the first seat she could find. It wasn't a non-smoking compartment, but it was only a ten-minute journey. I'm exhausted, Celia thought. She closed her eyes for a moment, thinking about the silky dress, dazzled for a second by a daydream of herself wearing it under one of those glass balls they had in dance halls, the kind that bounced darts of coloured light around the walls and on to the skin and hair of all the dancers . . . She opened her eyes.

'Do you mind if I smoke?' said the young man who was now sitting opposite her.

'No . . . not at all,' Celia said. Where on earth had he come from? How long, she wondered, have I been sitting here with my eyes closed? She glanced down at her watch – only a minute or so. He must have slipped in quietly. He's very polite. Fancy asking if I minded him smoking. Celia looked at him as he turned his head to look out of the window. Some kind of a soldier . . . some sort of uniform . . . very fair hair (dyed? thought Celia. You never knew, nowadays) but dark eyes . . . maybe blue, but dark. A parting in the hair . . . short at the back and sides and floppy at the front. As the train came into Birchwood, the young soldier stood up and smiled at Celia.

'Cheerio,' he said, and turned and walked down the compartment towards the door.

'Bye,' Celia said, still a little faint from the feelings

brought on by that smile. I can't run after him, she thought. I'll use the other door. She jumped on to the platform and looked for him . . . there he was, already over the bridge and on the other side. I should go after him, she thought. Call out to him. Being dignified and ladylike doesn't matter any more. What if I never see him again?

'Stop it!' Celia said aloud to herself, and then turned round to make sure she was alone. As she trudged over the bridge to where her father was waiting for her in the car, she told herself over and over again that she had only seen him for a few moments, that she would probably never see him again, and that she was being a fool. Nevertheless, she knew what it felt like to fall in love. It was as unmistakable as getting a cold, and she recognized within herself all the symptoms. The pain she felt at the very idea of never seeing him again made her want to cry. The headlights of her parents' car broke into a thousand small fragments of light in the tears she hadn't quite managed to blink away.

'I saw you on the train the other day, didn't I?'

'Yes, you asked if you could smoke,' Celia said. (Oh, glory be, here he is again . . . ten whole minutes . . . please, God, let the time go slowly . . . slow it down . . . let him like me . . . thank goodness I'm wearing the brown coat.)

'Well,' said the soldier, 'it's only polite to ask. I should introduce myself. My name's Neville . . .'

'Mine's Celia.'

'Delighted to meet you.'

What a funny way he has of talking, Celia thought. No one has ever said that to me . . . delighted to meet you.

'Do you live in Birchwood?'

'I do at the moment, of course,' Neville said. 'Based there, you know. Training.'

'Training for what?'

'Army, of course. Lots of chaps training up here, now.'

'Oh.' Celia was silent, racking her brains. She'd never seen any soldiers around Birchwood – she would certainly have noticed – but then, she'd only lived there a short time. Perhaps it was possible – maybe even a highly secret camp that no one was supposed to know about. Celia was bored by military matters and thought of a way to change the subject.

'Are you meeting someone in Manchester?' she asked.

'Yes, as a matter of fact. It's . . . well, it's a young lady.'

Neville blushed. Celia stared at him. She hardly knew anyone who blushed like that. She sighed. That's that, she thought. He's got a girlfriend. Wouldn't you know it? First time for six months I meet a decent bloke and someone else has got there first.

'Perhaps I'll see you again . . .' he said.

'Yeah,' Celia said. 'Bye.'

She muttered to herself as she walked towards the barrier: 'Forget him . . . forget him . . . he'll never be for you . . . he loves someone else.' As she left the station, she looked back towards the platform. Neville was still there, waiting. Hope she never shows up, Celia thought. Hope she's run away to Brazil with a second-hand car dealer. Hope she never comes back. I'll take care of Neville.

Celia looked at the lines of rain slanting across the window. Was that the same young woman, still waiting for someone? She was standing on the platform, waiting, but it was hard to see, through all that rain, who it was . . . The train pulled out of the station.

'It's Celia, isn't it?' A voice interrupted her thoughts.

'Hello, Mr Stockton. Fancy seeing you here.'

'It's a bit late for you, young lady, isn't it?'

'Not really. I often go home on this train after a film or something – Mum or Dad meet me. We'll give you a lift as well.'

'That'll be grand.' Mr Stockton sighed. 'On a night like this.'

Celia said, 'Those clothes you gave me . . . I hope you don't mind. I kept a coat and dress.'

Mr Stockton looked at Celia out of dark eyes.

'Mind, child? I'm delighted. Irene would have been delighted. She did think a lot of you, I know that. A properly brought-up child she said, not like some. And I'm glad someone young'll be wearing her things again. You look a little like her . . . she was thin . . . had the same colour hair, too. Fine, like a baby's it was – that soft. Eeh, I wish I had a pound for every time I've been up and down to Manchester on this line. I did my training up at Birchwood during the war, like many others, you know . . . oh yes . . . and backwards and fowards I used to go, to meet Irene in Manchester.'

'Did you go dancing?'

Mr Stockton chuckled. 'Yes, dancing, and to the cinema, and did a bit of spooning too . . .' He sighed. 'Same as you get up to with your young man, I've no doubt.'

'I haven't got a young man,' Celia said.

'You will have,' Mr Stockton said. 'There's no rush.'

Celia opened her mouth to tell him about Neville, then changed her mind.

'Nearly home now,' said Mr Stockton. 'There was a time when it was all aircraft noises round here. In the war.'

'You look . . . different tonight,' said Neville. 'I mean you look very smart, of course, and you remind me . . .'

'Yes?' Celia asked.

'Well, you remind me of someone.'

'Is it your friend? The young lady you're always going to meet?' Celia was dressed up for Forties Night at the Ritz in the silky dress and the brown woollen coat.

'Yes – yes, you look very much like her. Especially now. Have I told you that before?'

'Once or twice.'

Neville looked away.

'I'm sorry. You see, it's not that I don't . . . like you. I like you most awfully – I mean I *could* like you, but I have promised her . . .'

'But you say she's never there. Never at the station where she said she was going to be.' Celia's voice was full of anger. 'I hate to say this, but I think she's gone off you. I do really. Otherwise, why doesn't she turn up, eh? Honestly, Neville, face the facts. Please.'

The train was slowing down. The lights of the platform slipped past the window like bright beads. Celia stood up and Neville followed her.

'Celia!' Neville put out a hand, touched her sleeve.

'Yes?'

'You don't understand . . . I have to meet her . . . she's waiting for me . . . it's just that I have to find her . . . you can't possibly understand.'

'Don't talk about understanding,' Celia shouted. 'I'm fed up with it. Damn it, where's all your fine understanding? Can't you see that I love you? What do I have to do? Walk around with a sign on?'

Neville took Celia's face in his hands and kissed her softly on the mouth, so softly that she hardly felt it, and yet a shiver ran through her as if his lips had been ice-cold.

'I didn't know,' he said. 'I'm sorry. But I have to wait for her. I didn't know.'

The train stopped. Celia tore the door open, jumped out and ran towards the barrier. Through a fog of tears she could see Maddy.

'What's your rush?' Maddy said. 'You look as if you're running to save your life.'

56

'It's Neville. I'm fed up with him.'

'Ah, the mysterious unknown soldier. Let's get a squint at him. Where is he?'

'Up there, probably. That's where he usually is. Hanging about. Waiting for her.'

'Can't see a thing. Not a handsome soldier in sight anywhere. Come on, chuck, let's go and rustle up some grub, and then hit the Ritz with everything we've got.'

Maddy shimmied down the hill towards Oxford Road singing, asking innocent passers-by whether this was, indeed, the Chattanooga Choo-Choo. Celia followed her, stiff with misery.

'It isn't that bad, is it?' asked Maddy.

'It's terrible. All those people sweating, and everybody looking so – so . . .'

'So what?'

Celia sighed. 'So fleshy. So . . .' She could find no words.

Maddy put an arm around her shoulders. 'You don't mean any of that. You mean, they aren't this Neville of yours.'

'He's not "mine",' Celia said, 'He's someone else's. I'm sorry, Maddy. I'm going home. You and Graham stay. I'll be OK. Station's only across the road. Can you phone my mum and tell her I'm on the eleven-eighteen? I don't feel like talking to her . . . and I can't stand the music, Maddy, and that's the truth.'

'What's the matter with it? It's great.'

'It makes me feel like crying. All that stuff about

not knowing where and not knowing when, and the blue skies driving the dark clouds far away. I've never really thought before, what it must have been like . . .' she paused, 'to be in love with someone who could die at any moment, and to be in danger yourself.'

'Go home,' said Maddy. 'I can see what kind of mood you're in. And Graham's walking you up the hill, and I don't care what you say.'

'I'll go and get my coat,' Celia said.

Celia huddled against one of the pillars, trying not to be seen. The clock on the platform said eleven-fifteen. Three more minutes . . . oh, please, please, she thought, make him not look up. Make him not see me. She bit her lip and felt hope, any hope she had at all, drain out of every bit of her. Across the other platform she could see them quite clearly, standing under one of the lights. They stood close together. He had found her at last, his girl, the one he had been coming to meet all those other times. He was looking down at her – she seemed to fit herself into the circle of his arm, khaki against the brown fabric of her coat . . . A coat a lot like this, Celia thought, and glanced at them again. They had turned to leave now. Neville still had his arm fixed around the woman. It seemed to Celia that his arm was fixed there forever, that nothing could move it. At the barrier they stopped, and the woman stood on tiptoe so that he could kiss her. Celia watched them and felt sick. Where the hell was the train? She began to cry as it came into the station.

★

'Lovey,' said Celia's mother, 'what is it? What's happened? You surely can't have heard . . .'

'No, I'm fine . . . really . . . I just . . . it doesn't matter. Heard what?'

'About poor old Mr Stockton.'

'What about him?'

'He died. Just about half an hour ago, that's all.'

'How do you know?'

'Betty told me. She heard a crash. He pulled an armchair over as he fell. It was very quick. He can't have felt any pain. Poor thing! I feel sad. He hasn't any children or close family that we know of. I'll have to go over there and help Betty pack up his stuff. Tomorrow probably, or the next day. D'you want to give me a hand, love?'

'Might as well,' said Celia. I don't think I'll ever care strongly about anything ever again, she thought. My whole body feels like a mouth does after an injection at the dentist's. Numb, but with layers of pain hidden away, hidden deep down and far away.

The darkness makes you silly, Celia thought the next day. She and her mother and Betty, Mr Stockton's next door neighbour, were packing the old man's life away in cardboard boxes. Yesterday he was here, and now he isn't, she said to herself. Yesterday, when Neville kissed me in the corridor of the train, I thought there was a chance, a hope of something, and now I know there isn't. I should be able to pack the remains of what I feel into a box and give it to Oxfam. Get rid of it.

'How are you getting on?' Celia's mother shouted from the kitchen.

'Fine,' Celia yelled back. 'Just doing these albums . . .'

'Having a peep, are you?' Celia's mother came into the room.

'Can't help it. I'm nosey and I love all these old brown photos . . . only some of them are so small, you can hardly see what anybody looks like.'

'There's one fallen out, Celia. Be careful.'

Celia's mother bent to pick up the photograph. She smiled.

'This is a bit more like it. A bit bigger. Goodness, look at Irene Stockton on her wedding day! During the war, it must have been . . . he's in uniform. Registry Office wedding, of course . . . look how thin and pretty she was, and as for him, well, you'd never believe it was the same person as our Mr Stockton. Here, take it and push it in somewhere. I've got to get back to the kitchen . . .' Celia's mother left the room.

Celia sat looking at the photograph for a long time, and allowed herself to cry. Not for Mr Stockton, who had found his Irene at last, pretty in her silky, leafstrewn dress and brown woollen coat, nor for Neville, the young soldier Mr Stockton used to be, whose face smiled up at her now from the wedding photograph, but for her own mixture of regret and happiness: regret because she knew that she would never see him again, and happiness in discovering that love was indeed, as she had always suspected, stronger than death.

# The Centre

*From The Evening Gazette: October 25th*

**Manchester Police are mounting a city-wide hunt for young Stuart Windell (13), who disappeared last Saturday afternoon.**

### DISTRAUGHT

36-year-old Mrs Brenda Windell, the boy's mother, said this morning, 'We are all really distraught. This is not like Stuart at all. He went into town on Saturday to spend a record token. If anyone has seen him, please, please get in touch with the police. No one will be angry with him. We just want him back.'

### BAFFLED

Chief Inspector Frank Davis confessed himself baffled. 'We have interviewed Stuart's friends and scores of shoppers. Quite a few people think they remember seeing him in the Arndale Centre on Saturday afternoon.'

13-year-old Andrew Roberts, Stuart's best friend, told the Gazette reporter, 'Stu didn't catch the bus home with us. He said he was going to look around a bit. We didn't think anything of it. We just went home. I wish we hadn't now.'

### THIRD IN A SERIES?

Chief Inspector Davis refused to comment on the possibility that Stuart's disappearance was the third in a series of such happenings. A nationwide search has failed to find 10-year-old Elisabeth Lacey who was last seen on August 20th and there has been no news of 12-year-old Tracy Walsh, who vanished in May of this year.

### IS THE CENTRE SAFE?

All three children were last seen at the Arndale Centre, which prompts the Evening Gazette to ask: is the Centre really safe, in spite of police presence during the daytime and a regular night patrol? (*See page 6 for Editorial comment.*)

The Desk Sergeant had recognized Ted the minute he'd walked into the station: old Ted Rees, four layers of clothes on top of countless layers of dirt and the whole lot walking along in a fog of stale booze and cigarettes.

'. . . a word with . . . Chief Inspector Davis . . . That's right,' he was saying.

The young policeman sighed and looked as severely as he could at the old tramp standing before him. 'Ted,' he said. 'I'm sure you've got a lot to say to the Chief, but now's not the time. We're busy, see? Got a lot on our plates, know what I mean? Whyn't you go back to the Centre where you belong and have a look at the televisions in Philip's window? Go on, there's a good chap.'

Ted sniffed, shuffled his feet and muttered, 'Been watching it, haven't I? Why I'm here. That, and the paper, like. Gissa fag, Sarge, and I'll tell you. Doesn't have to be the Chief. Tell you all about it.'

'Let's be having it then,' said the policeman. 'Got nothing on at all, I haven't. Just ready for a bedtime story, I am. Go on, I'm sitting comfortably . . .'

'What about the fag though? Can't think right at this time of day, not without a smoke.'

'Don't smoke, though, do I? Filthy habit. Come on, either you tell your tale and get out or you just get out. Which is it going to be?'

Ted hesitated, turned to go.

'Don't know if I'll bother . . . wanted to see the Chief, really, like . . . about that kid . . . the one that's gone missing . . .'

No magician uttering abracadabra ever effected a speedier transformation. The Desk Sergeant shot out from behind his desk, and within five minutes, Ted Rees found himself sitting at a table drinking a cup of tea and eating digestive biscuits. Across the table from him was the Chief: Chief Inspector Frank Davis himself.

'Grand,' Ted chuckled. 'That was grand. Do a nice cuppa tea in this nick, I'll say that for you. You haven't got a fag on you, have you? Finish the tea off a treat, a fag would.'

Chief Inspector Davis threw a packet of cigarettes and a box of matches down on to the table.

'Use your saucer for an ashtray. And start talking. I haven't got all day, you know.'

Ted smiled. 'Ain't half long, these fags aren't. When they're not dog-ends. Used to dog-ends, meself.'

'I'm sorry I couldn't get you any then,' Chief Inspector Davis muttered through clenched teeth. 'Now. Let's be having you. You seen the boy, or what?'

'No. Ain't seen him. He's gone, in't he? No one's seen him. That's the point.'

'Then what the bloody hell are you wasting police time for? Thought you said you had information, you dirty old bundle of rubbish. Get out, go on, get out.'

'I never said I hadn't got information. Only that I hadn't seen him. I have got information . . .'

Chief Inspector Davis sighed. 'Start at the beginning.'

'Right,' Ted coughed. 'D'you remember what used

to be there down Market Street before they put up that Centre?'

'Shops,' the Chief Inspector said. 'What's this got to do with anything?'

'I'm coming to that.' Ted picked a digestive crumb from his beard and chewed it thoughtfully. 'Do you remember Clevely's?'

'Clevely's? Dress shop, or drapers or what have you? I must have walked past it a thousand times I suppose. What about it?'

'Ever met Ma Clevely, what ran it?'

'No, and I don't care if I never do. Listen, mate, if you think you're going to sit there puffing at your bleeding Bensons and gossiping about shopkeepers, you've got another think coming . . .'

'Keep your hair on . . . it's all . . . what's that word . . . revelant.'

'Relevant.'

'Yes. Relevant. Just listen while I tell you. This Ma Clevely was a terror. Had a lot of young girls out at the back of the shop, sewing away for dear life. Sweated labour, it was. I say she was a terror, 'cos she's dead. Them closing her shop and all. Putting up that pile of shoeboxes, that's what did for her. Mind, she was old. I'm not saying she wasn't. I can remember a time, before you were born, oh yes, when all the gentry, all the ladies went there for dresses and suits and such. They had kiddies' clothes too. I had a top hat from there once.'

'You never had a top hat in your life, you old fraud.'

Ted glared at the Chief Inspector. 'Didn't get born a tramp, though, did I? What do you know about it anyway? But Ma Clevely . . . they had to throw her out, you know. It was in the papers. But I saw it. They chucked out all the dummies and stuff, clothes and that, into the van that was waiting on the pavement, and she was stood there screaming. Saying she'd be back. Saying she'd have her shop again, ranting and raving like she was drunk . . .'

'Is this getting us anywhere?' Chief Inspector Davis had stopped making notes.

'I'm coming to what I want to say . . . This is it . . .' He paused and took the cigarette out of his mouth, and leaned forward.

'I reckon she's back there. Back in that Centre.'

'I thought you said she was dead . . .'

'She is . . .'

'What's this then? You've seen her ghost? Is that it? You've been wasting everyone's time with a spooky little story out of your drink-fuddled brain. Go on, get out of here. Just go. I've had enough.'

Ted Rees stood up. 'I haven't seen her. But I can tell, Chief. She's there, all right. And I reckon it's her what took them kids.'

'And what's she supposed to have done with them? Set them sewing invisible clothes on invisible machines in a bloody non-existent shop? Go on, clear off out of here before I book you as drunk and disorderly.'

It was drizzling as Ted Rees left the Police Station and made his way back to the Arndale Centre. No drizzle in there, he thought. No air, no sunshine, but no drizzle either. There was that much to be said for it.

'Do we have to go, Mum?' Sharon Windell hesitated at the door. 'Do we really have to?'

'Do you think I like it any better than you? Don't you think I'd rather stay away when it all reminds me of him . . .?' Brenda Windell sniffed. 'But I've got no choice, have I? I'm not getting you a coat somewhere else when I've got ten pounds credit at Brink's, am I?'

'No, I suppose not.' Sharon sighed as they left the house. 'Anyway,' she said, 'maybe this time we'll . . .'

'No, Sharon, we won't.' Her mother shook her head. 'I used to think like that. Every phone call, every knock at the door, I used to hope and pray, but now it's nearly a month and I've stopped hoping . . . someone would have seen him if he were alive . . .'

Sharon thought: but if he were dead, there'd be his body, wouldn't there? I don't believe it. I don't believe he's dead. They can all say what they like, the police and everything, but if he were dead, I'd know. I'd feel it inside. And I don't. There's an emptiness inside me. If Stu were dead there wouldn't be an emptiness. There'd be a hurt, an awful hurt like claws, tearing me.

Walking through the Arndale Centre with her mother, Sharon felt that nothing in it was real. For a start, there was no real light, only a bluish brightness about the air that sucked the colour from people's cheeks so that everyone looked pale. The light never

66

changed either, not like outside. There, it was sunny or dull, day or night, dawn, sunset, moonlight even, and here – nothing: a pale neon nothing, the kind of light that didn't even make shadows. The air smelled of plastic. Cold and heat never penetrated the Centre. Neither did rain or sunshine. What you heard was noise, but no voices. Disembodied loudspeaker announcements, frantic music spilling out of shops, the same tired water being pumped up out of the fountains, splashing half-heartedly on to rubbery plants. Sharon set herself to count the people who were smiling. She didn't see any, unless she was going to include the shrieking bands of boys and girls not much older than Stu, trying to look as if they were having a good time, making the walkways ring to the clatter of their hard, hard shoes. Later, sitting with her mother on a yellow plastic bench, looking at the people walking by, she was suddenly struck by their sameness. It was as though every time she came here the identical crowd was waiting for her. They belonged to the Centre, Sharon decided. They were a part of it, not real people from outside at all, just a breed of mechanical Centre-people who lived there, stayed there always, a part of it. As much a part of it as the escalators and the litter bins and the wooden animals for the children to climb on. And Stu had become one of them, she was sure of it. The more she thought about it, the more plausible it seemed to her. He had been absorbed by the Centre, sucked in to become one of its people. That was why no one had found his body: because he was here. Here where she was. And if she looked carefully, she realized with a sudden racing of the heart, she might find him . . .

'Mum, can we walk about a bit more? I want to look at the shops.'

'Really? I thought you hated this place. I know I do. Still, if you want to . . .'

They walked and walked and Sharon peered at every face as she passed it. There was no sign of her brother. But I know he's here, she thought, as they made their way out of the Centre and into the street. I'll go and tell the police. They'll know what to do.

'Well now, Sharon.' Chief Inspector Davis smiled his 'I'm-being-kind-to-a-child' smile. 'That's all very interesting, you know, but I assure you it's not true. You see, dear, we've checked everything. Already. And I promise you, at the end of every day, everyone leaves the Centre and the whole place is locked up and there's only the night-watchman. Really. I wouldn't lie to you, now would I?'

Sharon shook her head.

'Now I'll get my sergeant to take you home in a police car, Sharon. How would you like that?'

'No, you mustn't. I mean, thanks, but I'll take the bus. My mum doesn't know I've come to see you. She thinks I'm at Francine's house. Thanks for the drink.'

After she had gone, Chief Inspector Davis shook his head in amazement. The things these kids came up with. Honestly. Whatever next . . . all the people in the Centre not real . . . it's television that's responsible,

68

he thought. Feed them a lot of imaginary rubbish and here's what happens. Can't sort out what's real and what isn't. Still (Chief Inspector Davis prided himself on his awareness of modern psychology), the poor little kid had been under a lot of strain, what with her brother gone missing and liable to turn up dead one day. Perhaps it made it easier to think . . . anything at all.

Sharon hid in the belly of the huge wooden rhino and waited. She was nervous, but it was a good plan and she had to carry it through or she would never know . . . Francine was in the plan. She's my alibi, thought Sharon. I'm supposed to be spending the night at her house. Francine's mum and dad are going out tonight. Right at this very minute the baby-sitter thinks I'm up in Francine's room . . . we made a shape out of pillows to put in the other bed. We practised. I'll go back first thing in the morning. I wonder what time they open this place up . . . Sharon looked at her watch. Eight o'clock. She peeped out of the rhino. The Centre was empty. All the big lights had been turned off, but shop lights still shone out on to the marble. The silence filled her ears, deafened her. She had heard the night-watchman earlier, walking about, but he had gone now. That was one good thing about marble floors – you could hear someone coming from a long way away, and going back to wherever they came from as well. No one would hear her though. She had worn her trainers especially.

She climbed down out of the rhino, and began to

walk slowly along a walkway that seemed to stretch on forever, staying very close to the shop windows, as if the colourless light could banish the fear, as if the models inside could reach out plastic arms for comfort. The fountains had been turned off. The plants were black near the black water. Twice, she heard the night-watchman and hid behind a bench and looked at him. He seemed very old and frail to be a guard. Just an old man, really, but it pleased her that he was there somewhere, ready to give help if she needed it. Another human being in a desert of stone and half-light and silence. Sharon crept down the unmoving escalator to that part of the Centre which lay below ground level. She and her mother hardly ever came down here: all the big stores were upstairs, but Sharon felt she had to look everywhere. I won't find anything, she thought. I must be mad. Chief Inspector Davis was right. All the people who come here are ordinary people and they all go home at night to their houses and there's nothing here at all but silence and this dim light and shops . . . and those animals and the night-watchman. She leaned her forehead against a shop window and something caught her eye. It was a shoe. A trainer, just like Stu's. The dummy in the window was wearing trainers just like Stu's. She shivered. There was nothing strange about that. Perhaps the shop sold trainers. She looked more closely. It couldn't be. It was. A pink stain on the white part of the shoe, like the stain she'd made spilling Ribena on Stu's trainers the first week he'd had them. She would never forget his anger, nor the shape of the mark that was left after Mum had scrubbed them: like a lopsided heart. A crooked heartshaped stain and there it was right in front of her in the window. She raised her eyes a little, hardly daring to look . . . and there he was, or a dummy that was dressed in his clothes . . . Sharon pressed herself up against the window to see better. They were Stu's clothes, she was sure of that. And the dummy . . . the dummy looked like her brother. How had they done it? Why? Who would want to? And where was Stu if this model boy was wearing his clothes? Sharon knew at once what she had to do – get into the shop and get the clothes off the plastic limbs of that doll and take them to the police. They'd know. They'd have tests they could do to show that the clothes were Stu's. I'll have to break the glass, she thought, and then: if I do, I'll get into trouble. I'd better find the night-watchman, call out to him, he'll understand. Everyone will understand when they see what I've found. Mum and Dad and Francine's parents – no one will be cross. These are clues. This will help them find out what's happened to Stu. She glanced at the dummy again and was just plucking up courage to shout into all the silence and break it, when she heard the footsteps far away and dived into the tiny space of the shop doorway, flattening herself against the glass, her heart beating so loudly that the pulse filled her head. The sound of the footsteps was nearer now. Tap, tap, swish. Tap, tap, swish on the marble like a lady in a long, silky dress. It can't be, Sharon thought. It's the night-watchman. And I want him to come. I do. I was going to call him. Closer . . . tap, tap, swish . . . and closer. Sharon left the doorway and stepped out to see who was coming. High-ceilinged passages stretched away to both sides of her . . . she could see and see and see for what looked like miles. No one. Nothing at all. Just a sound. Tap, tap, swish . . . closer and closer. Louder and louder.

'Who is it?' Sharon tried to scream, but it came out a croak, almost a whisper. 'What do you want? Who are you?' Her own voice bounced back from the silence all around her. 'There's a night-watchman, you know. He'll get you! He will . . . Help!'

Tap, tap, swish. Nearer. Almost on top of her. Darkness came down over Sharon's eyes and she turned and ran. She didn't know where she was running to . . . part of her mind knew she must find the guard, yell and scream, attract attention, but her body said run, hide, keep silent, get away, escape.

At her back the footsteps gathered speed. She could hear hoarse panting behind her, almost at her shoulder, and she ran and ran, blindly, thinking only of the unmoving silver escalator, thinking of getting up, up, out of this underground place, away from the terrible swishing and the laboured breathing . . . away anywhere. There it was. The escalator. Sharon lunged towards it and almost flew up the steps. At the top, she stumbled and fell. Can't fall. Get up. Can't stop. It's coming. Get up. Coming nearer. Up. Sharon crawled to her feet and began to run again, half-covering her eyes with her hands because she couldn't bear to look again and see nothing. Up here. The watchman must be here. Sharon found her voice.

72

'Stop it. Please help . . . help me . . .' Sound tore itself from her throat, which was blocked and filled with terror and the exhaustion of running and running and not stopping for breath.

'Where are you? Please . . . I'm sorry for being here . . . please. Come and save me . . . Oh, I can't . . . I can't run any more.'

But she ran, because it was there . . . tap, tap, swish . . . so near. Not a swish, a rustle. Like petticoats . . . so close now. And breathing and something else. A smell, like old face powder . . . old perfume . . . stale, stale and old . . . horrible. Run, fly away, hide. Where to hide in all the marble and the glass? The rhino, Sharon thought. I must get to the rhino. There it was. Wooden. Hollow. Somewhere to hide till someone comes. She ran, stumbled, crawled along, unable to breathe properly any more, until she reached it. Her head was full of footsteps and rustling and in her nostrils the smell . . . stronger now. Violets. It made her want to vomit. She fell against the smooth wooden feet of the rhino and climbed into the opening of its belly. There was a small platform inside. Sharon curled up with her hands wrapped round her head to shut out the sounds, and her knees touching her face, breathing in her own smell, the smell of her jeans and her own sweat, trying to blot out that other smell . . . Minutes passed. Sharon listened. Silence. No more footsteps. I'll wait, she thought, and then I'll look. I'll look out of the top. She lay trembling, crying, cold with fear for ten minutes timed on her watch, and then she slowly uncurled and stood up . . . at once the smell flew up at her face, stronger than ever, as if it were a live thing lying in wait for her outside the rhino's body. She ducked down and curled up again on the platform, pressing herself against the wood, wishing she could become a part of it, melt into it, stop being herself, disappear, dissolve . . . The wooden walls all round her seemed softer, wrapped her and enfolded her, and in her ear came a whisper . . . sleep, sleep, and Sharon closed her eyes. Sleep . . . forget . . . don't run away any more, don't hide any more, just sleep. Close your eyes and sleep. Sleep and dream. Dream.

This is a dream. I know it is, because everything is wavy. The air is rippling like water, breaking into patterns, swirls of light and shadow and nothing is hard. Even wood is soft, like flesh . . . and I'm not afraid. Hands, gloved hands are touching me, gentle hands. I'm being pulled out of somewhere . . . lifted, yes, like a baby . . . arms are lifting me, but I can't feel the arms . . . carrying me. I can hear somebody walking . . . tap, tap, swish . . . and smell violets . . . lovely . . . soft, powdery smell. Looking up. I'm looking up and lights are slipping by over my head slowly, and slowly and then more quickly, and then no more lights. Darkness and a bed . . . or a table, with a sheet on it, and then someone is stroking me, like a cat, stroking . . . a cat's tail, but it's wet . . . stroking my arms and my feet and in between my fingers, and my face . . . wetness all over my face . . . lips, nose, cheeks all wet. I want to touch my face but my arm is heavy.

I can't move it. I want to turn my head. My head won't turn. I'm stiff. All stiff and cold. I can't move at all. Only my eyes. Hands lift me. I can't feel hands, but I'm lifted. Standing. The light is white ... eyes hurt ... can't move head. No more moving ... don't need to move. Stuart is next to me. He can't move. But we can see. See each other. Not move, but see each other always. Stay like this. Stiff. Always.

Ted Rees looked at the photograph in the newspaper and sighed. He looked at it again and then threw it away in the litter bin. Poor little thing. First the brother and now her. I've seen her before somewhere. Where, though, that's the thing? Where was it now? It's hard to remember, but I seen her. Ma Clevely's got her, that's what. Bloody coppers. She's here, 'cos I heard her and I smelled her and I know and she's got her. All of them, probably, and I seen them, but I don't know ... it's hard to remember. Poor little kid ... Poor Ted ... maybe when I get sober I'll remember again ... never know yer luck.

The old tramp propped himself against the shop window and looked in. Then he started laughing. Choking and laughing and coughing and making such a noise that the Centre policeman was forced to give him a warning.

'Come on, Ted. Can't have this row, you know. Scares everyone off, doesn't it? Can't see what's so bleeding funny anyhow.'

'It's him, see. That boy doll in that window. He's

got a wine stain on that fancy shoe of his. Just like me. I got one and all. Wanna have a look?'

The policeman led Ted away, still laughing.

# Captain Ashe's Daughter

Every Thursday afternoon at 2.30, Bridget Carney presented herself at Holmecroft Old People's Home and made her way across the beige carpet in the Sun Lounge to where Sybil Meadows always sat. Sybil was one of Holmecroft's oldest residents and very proud of her status.

'I'm as old as the century,' she told Bridget on her very first visit. 'Ninety-four next birthday and I've never been further than Blackpool all my life. And what's more . . .' (she raised her voice so that no one should miss what she was about to say) 'I might be weak, but I've still got all my marbles, unlike some old fossils I could mention!'

That was true. 'Sybil's quite a character,' Matron had said. 'Got the gift of the gab, that one, and no mistake. Start her off on a story and there's no stopping her.'

Bridget thought Sybil was a little cheeky, speaking as she did about all the other old folks. At first, the sight of so many elderly people together in one room, nodding, trembling, staring at you curiously, was a little unnerving, but Bridget had grown used to coming to Holmecroft and most of the time she enjoyed her afternoons with Sybil.

Bridget's visits were part of her Sixth Form College's 'Care in the Community' Scheme. She had undertaken to read to Sybil for a couple of hours every Thursday afternoon but when she'd volunteered, she'd imagined novels, stories, anything from Charles Dickens to Mills and Boon. She had certainly never thought that the *South Manchester Reporter* was going to be what Sybil wished to hear. There wasn't anything wrong with the *South Manchester Reporter*, but when you'd read every single letter (about wheelie bins, muggers, Pets' Corner in Fog Lane Park, etc, etc) and every single local news item, including most of the advertising copy and what was showing at Cinecity this week, you did begin to long for narrative of some kind. Next week, Bridget vowed to herself as she turned over to page four, I'll suggest a book. Maybe I'll bring one. I'll ask Gran what she likes.

'Cat got your tongue, Bridget?' Sybil asked. 'Why aren't you reading?'

'Just turning over, Miss Meadows,' said Bridget. 'Here we go: "Didsbury mansion bought by Computer Firm." That's the headline. "Willow Grange, once the home of cotton merchant Isaac Winterthorne, has been standing empty for some time now . . ."'

'Stop!' said Sybil. 'Did you say Willow Grange?'

'Yes.'

'Oh my,' said Sybil, almost whispering. 'Willow Grange. I thought I'd left that far, far behind me, and now here it is again.'

'Do you know the house?' Bridget asked.

'Know it? Oh, yes. I was there almost from the beginning. The house had just been built. I went into service at Willow Grange when I was fourteen years old. The war had just started. I mean the First War, of course. The Great War. It was supposed to be over by Christmas, you know, but it wasn't. I was to be parlourmaid, only Miss Isabel, who was Isaac Winterthorne's daughter, took a fancy to me, and wanted to train me as her lady's maid. I'd never seen a house like Willow Grange before . . . not from the inside. There were floors with parquet tiles on them like satin (and they need a lot of polishing, I can tell you that!) and chandeliers that hung down from the ceiling, and all those little tinkly crystal bits needed dusting, and once a year Johnson, the butler, used to take them down with a special gadget that had a hook on the end of it. We spent hours washing the dratted things. Then there were the Turkey rugs to be shaken out (no Hoovers, my dear, not in 1914) and meals seemed to take all day, what with cooking them, serving them, and washing up afterwards. Still, I was happy at Willow Grange. I had a black dress and a white pinafore, and the Winterthornes were good to me, when they noticed I was there. Best of all, though, there was Miss Isabel. We took to one another straight

79

away. She was only a few years older than me ...
seventeen when I arrived at the house, and she'd chat
to me as I brushed her hair or tidied her room, just as
if I were her sister. We used to take walks around the
garden after lunch. I'd never seen a garden like that,
not before I went there, and not often since. I was
born in a street where the red-brick houses were built
back-to-back, and if you saw a tree once a year, you
counted yourself lucky. The garden at Willow Grange
was a paradise: banks of rhododendron so thick that
you couldn't see the back of the house from the street,
and lawns like the baize on the master's billiard table
in the Games Room and the flowerbeds full of rose-
bushes with never a leaf out of place, and borders full
of such colours, and butterflies on all the shrubs in
summer, and of course, the artificial lake.'

'They mention a lake,' said Bridget. 'In the article.
Listen: "The original owner had an ornamental lake
made in the grounds, and the willow trees which
were planted around it gave the house its name."'

'That's true enough,' said Sybil, 'but lake's a bit too
big a word, to my mind. It was more of a pond
really. In the Japanese style. It was full of waterlilies,
and there was a little wooden bridge over the water
that Miss Isabel and I used to like to stand on. On
really sunny days you could see the goldfish, swim-
ming about among the tangled roots of the
waterlilies.'

'Where is this Willow Grange?' Bridget asked. 'I've
never seen it.'

'Oh, well, it was always well-hidden. There's lots

of houses in Didsbury not everybody knows about. Willow Grange is behind Barlow Moor Road, down by the Mersey. You'd never find it if you weren't looking.'

'Why hasn't it been lived in for so long?' Bridget wanted to know. 'If it's so posh and everything?'

Sybil stared into space for such a long time that Bridget was on the point of calling for Matron. Then she said quietly, 'It wouldn't surprise me a bit if that place was haunted.'

'You're not serious!' Bridget laughed. 'You don't mean ghosts, do you? Your actual white floaty kind?'

'There's ghosts and ghosts,' Sybil said. 'All I know is, after what happened Mr and Mrs Winterthorne didn't fancy living there any more and who could blame them?'

'What *did* happen? Do tell me,' said Bridget.

'What about the rest of my newspaper, though?' Sybil asked. 'When'll I hear that?'

'This is more exciting than anything in the paper, honestly.'

'Exciting? Perhaps. The Winterthornes left Willow Grange and after that it became some kind of school, and then an old people's home, but nothing ever lasted very long there, and lately, well ... I hadn't heard anything about it for years and years and I'd forgotten all about it, you might say, only forgotten is the wrong word. I remember everything perfectly, only I've pushed it to the back of my mind, so as not to have to think about it too much. I do dream about it sometimes, though.'

Bridget suppressed a sigh. At this rate, dragging the story out of Sybil was going to take hours and hours.

'Tell me all about it,' she said encouragingly. 'I'm longing to hear what happened. How did it begin?'

'I suppose,' said Sybil, 'it began with the grey cat. This cat seemed to come from nowhere. We caught sight of it one day in the garden. It was sitting on the terrace outside the French windows looking at us. It was a thin creature, but big. Grey all over, and with such smooth short fur that it looked from certain angles almost hairless. It had huge amber eyes that stared and stared. Miss Isabel was never a lover of cats, it's true, but she took against this one in a way that was a little . . .' Sybil paused, trying to find the right word, 'excessive. That's it. Excessive. The first time she saw it, she sprang up from her seat on one of the garden benches and gave a cry of horror.

'"Oh, Sybil," she shivered. "Get rid of it. Please get rid of it."

'I stood up too, and began to say "shoo" and clap my hands in the general direction of the cat. It didn't move. It didn't flinch. I don't think it even blinked, but simply continued gazing at us with those enormous amber eyes. Then Miss Isabel did something quite unlike her. She was the calmest and gentlest of young ladies, and very dignified, but she knelt down and picked up two handfuls of gravel. Then she approached the cat and threw both handfuls of small stones straight at it as hard as she could throw. Her face was quite red from the effort, and she sat down on the garden bench again, shaking and trembling in every limb. The cat fled, of course, stung by the hail of tiny hard stones, but at the edge of the lawn he turned round, and fixing Miss Isabel with an unblinking gaze, he opened his mouth and hissed at her, showing sharp white teeth. Then he found a place in the shadow of a rhododendron, and sat there on his haunches, unmoving.

'He was always there after that. He never lay down. He never seemed to close his eyes. He never approached us, Miss Isabel and me, as we walked round the garden, but we felt him looking at us wherever we went. Miss Isabel couldn't bear it. After a while, she stopped walking in the garden altogether, but that didn't help. The cat came nearer and nearer to the house then, sometimes sitting right outside the French windows and staring in, and sometimes jumping up on to the outside windowsills, and pressing his nose against the glass, so that his breath misted the window. And then, one terrible day (oh, I'll never forget that day!) the cat found its way into the house, and into Miss Isabel's bedroom.

'The first I knew about it was the screaming. I was in the kitchen when I heard it, and I realized at once that it was Miss Isabel. I ran upstairs and the screams continued. It was like nothing else I've ever heard before or since, a noise like something tearing, or being torn apart. By the time I reached the bedroom door, it was already open and Miss Isabel's parents were there, comforting her, holding her, soothing her.

'"Fetch hot water, Sybil, quickly!" Mrs Winterthorne said to me. "And bandages. Run now."

83

'Miss Isabel's gown was torn. Her hands were covered in long, scarlet scratches dotted with drops of blood. Later, after she had calmed down, she told me, as well as she was able to, what had happened. The cat was on her bed. It wouldn't move. She clapped her hands at it. She flapped her shawl at it, but it stayed there as though it had grown roots that fastened it to the bedspread. Miss Isabel couldn't explain why she did what she did next. She went to pick up the cat, thinking to put it outside her door at least, but it began to struggle, and to claw at Miss Isabel's hands and the sleeves of her gown. She threw it away from her, not realizing how *frantic* she was, what unaccustomed strength was in her arms. The cat flew across the room, catching its back leg on the corner of the chest-of-drawers.

'"I think I hurt its leg," Miss Isabel told me. "It limped out of the room, dragging its leg behind it . . . oh, it was dreadful . . . and it looked at me with those terrible eyes as it went, and it was hissing. I can't bear it, Sybil, I can't bear it. What will I do if it comes back?"

'I told her it wouldn't come back, though of course I had no idea whether it would or not, but I had to calm her down, somehow. I had to cheer her up. I changed the subject. I began to talk about the following evening, when the Winterthornes were entertaining several local families to dinner and cards. Our conversation turned to dresses and hair ornaments, and slowly Miss Isabel became quieter. By the time I left her to go to my room in the attic, she was quite herself.'

'What about the cat?' Bridget asked. 'What happened to him?'

'We never laid eyes on him again. But the very next evening, Isabel met Captain Ashe and that was that.'

'What do you mean: that was that?'

'I mean,' said Sybil, 'that her fate was sealed from the moment she laid eyes on him. There was not a force in the universe that could have kept them apart.' Sybil held up her two hands and brought them together with the fingers intertwined and locked together. 'It was like watching something being drawn toward a magnet.' Sybil smiled. 'Captain Ashe was the most extraordinary-looking man: tall, slim, smooth with pale blond hair and strange yellowy-brown eyes. It was in my mind as soon as I saw him that his eyes were just like those of the grey cat, but Miss Isabel clearly liked him, and I didn't think I should draw the resemblance to her attention.'

'Did you think he *was* the grey cat, changed in some mysterious way into a man? Come back to get his revenge on Isabel who had been so cruel to him?'

Sybil laughed. 'I *did* think that . . . but I quickly told myself off for being a silly ignorant girl. How could such things go on in a modern sort of world? But still, I had nightmares about Captain Ashe. In my dreams he had a limp. He was dragging his left foot behind him, only of course it wasn't a human foot at all, but a cat's paw sticking out of the khaki trouser leg . . . oh, it gives me the shudders even now to think of it!'

'What happened then?'

'Well, Miss Isabel and Captain Ashe became engaged, and then married and we all thought that everything would be happy ever after, just like in the fairytales, but we had counted without the war. It had been decided that until the conflict was over, Miss Isabel (I couldn't help but keep calling her that, even though she wasn't a Miss any longer) should stay at home. We grew very close as the months passed. The Captain was in France and every day that went by without us seeing his name on the casualty lists we counted as a happy one. Miss Isabel confided in me as we knitted socks for the troops ... how much she loved him ... how much she missed him. And ... you have to remember that in those days we were not so free and easy about sex in our conversation, as all you young people are. She never said so directly, of course, but I understood from all kinds of hints she dropped that ... well, that they were well-suited to one another. I shan't say more than that.

'Then, towards the end of 1916, the Captain came home. He had been wounded. His left foot, just as I had dreamed it. The bandages were covered by a grey sock ... oh, I trembled when I saw him, limping across the hall, that first day. Miss Isabel's face when she caught sight of him would have done as a lamp, it was that happy.'

Sybil fell silent. She shook her head.

'Do go on,' said Bridget. 'What happened next?'

'The Captain had changed. He was quiet and moody at first and then he stopped speaking alto-

86

gether. This was bad enough of course, but we had all heard what the fighting did to the young men who had been in it, and we made allowances. It was decided that until the Captain had quite recovered, he and Miss Isabel should continue to make Willow Grange their home. Mr and Mrs Winterthorne forgave him everything, but I was the one who helped Miss Isabel to dress and undress and I could forgive him nothing.

'"Don't say a word, Sybil," Miss Isabel begged me, seeing my eyes open at the bruises all over her lovely white skin. One day, I noticed scratches round her wrists, but I said nothing. In the end, after several weeks, Isabel spoke to her parents. There were lights burning in the study until very late at night, and the next day Captain Ashe left the house forever. I saw him limping down the drive, and at the gate he turned and looked straight up at Miss Isabel's window. Perhaps he thought I was Miss Isabel. In any case, he smiled and I saw his sharp white teeth and the yellow light shining out of his eyes.'

'So Isabel was happy after all . . .'

'Not for long. It soon became clear that she was expecting a baby.

'"How can I?" she used to say to me, and I would answer, "The child will remind you of better times. Of the days when you still loved the Captain. After all, the baby won't have been changed by the war. It'll be the *real* Captain Ashe's child . . . will it be a boy or a girl, I wonder?"

'Over the months of her pregnancy, Miss Isabel

grew gradually happier. We stopped knitting socks and turned our efforts to tiny garments. Then the baby was born, a lovely girl, with almond-shaped eyes of a colour that reminded everyone of her father, and a soft golden down on her head. She was a pretty little thing. I hadn't much experience of babies, but everyone said how unusual her eyes were, and how they weren't the dull blue of most newborn infants, and how they seemed to look right through you. Miss Isabel called her Elizabeth. Bessie.

'When Bessie was three days old, my own mother took sick, and I was sent for to go and nurse her. I was away for four days. As soon as I returned, even before I'd knocked at the door, I knew something terrible had happened. The curtains had been pulled across all the windows. Someone had died.

'"Is it Miss Isabel?" I asked Johnson, who opened the door to me.

'"No," he answered. "She's in her room. I doubt they'll let you see her. The doctor's been."

'"But why are all the curtains drawn? Who is dead?"

'"It's the baby. Little Bessie."

'I didn't wait to hear any more, but flew upstairs to be at Miss Isabel's side. When Mrs Winterthorne saw me, she said, "Oh, Sybil, my dear. Thank goodness you are here." Her eyes were scarlet with weeping. "Speak to her. Comfort her."

'I persuaded Mrs Winterthorne to go and lie down, now that I was here. When she had gone, I sat beside Miss Isabel. She was pale and looked tired, but seemed very calm.

'"Sybil," she said. "You will believe me, will you not?"

'"Yes, Miss Isabel."

'"Because I've never lied to you. They are coming tomorrow to take me to an Institution. You know what that means, Sybil. But at least my parents will not call the police. An empty coffin will be buried. I shall cheat the hangman."

'I burst into tears. I couldn't help it. The shock was too much.

'"Why?" I cried. "What has happened?"

'"I killed her," Miss Isabel said quietly. "I took her down to the lake and held her under the water until she was dead. I had to."

'"Why?" I asked. "Why did you have to?"

'Miss Isabel turned placid blue eyes upon me.

'"Because," she said clearly, "Bessie was turning into a cat. I heard her quite plainly, purring in her cot. The sound was almost deafening. Such things cannot be allowed to exist ... such monstrosities. I had to drown her. I loved her, you see. You do see, don't you? No one else understands. I had to . . ."

Sybil's voice faltered. She could hardly speak for crying.

'I'm so sorry,' said Bridget. 'I never meant the story to upset you. It's so sad. What happened after that?'

'Miss Isabel was sent abroad to a sanatorium. I was given my notice. The Winterthornes sold the house and left the area. I tried to put the whole thing out of my mind or I would have ended up in the madhouse as well. I never went near the house again, although over the years I've heard stories about it. There's something crying in the night. It could be a baby, or perhaps a cat. No one stays long in the house though. Let's leave the paper now, dear, shall we? I'm not in the mood for news any longer. You can come and tell me the latest again next week.'

On the following Thursday, Bridget hurried to Holmecroft with the newspaper. She could scarcely wait to tell Sybil the news.

'I'm so terribly sorry, dear,' said the Matron. 'Sybil passed away two days ago.'

'But she can't have,' Bridget burst out.

'She was ninety-three, dear,' said the Matron. 'It was a long, happy life. She died very peacefully.'

'I wanted to . . .' Bridget started to say, and changed her mind. There was no point.

When she got home, she cut the small paragraph out of the newspaper, as a souvenir. She read it again.

## KIND WORKMEN BURY OLD BONES

Last Friday morning, workmen busy on the site of the ornamental lake at Willow Grange came across the bones of what is thought to be a small cat. The police were called in, but gave permission for the remains to be disposed of.

'It looked so sad,' said foreman Mr Michael Raines, 'that we decided to bury it properly. We put all the bones we could find under a pink rhododendron bush, and said a few prayers. Perhaps it was a family pet that fell into the lake and got entangled in the waterlily roots or something. We all hope the poor little thing will rest in peace.'

Amen, thought Bridget. Amen.

# Burning Memories

The second thing my dad did when he heard that he'd got the job at Cedar House was buy me this notebook I'm writing in now as a celebration present. I've never had anything fancier than a red exercise book before, but this is a proper journalist's notebook, only with pretty flowers on the cover, the kind that makes you want to write down everything that's happening so that you won't ever forget it, and also all your secret thoughts.

The first thing Dad did when we came out of Cedar House after the interview was leap into the air, clicking the heels of his boots together, and shout 'Yee-hah!' My dad shouts 'Yee-hah!' whenever he feels at all pleased, but it's usually a quiet sort of shout. This wasn't. This was a really raucous and triumphant 'Yee-haah!!!' which startled some ladies who were on their way to the posh shops in Didsbury.

I don't expect they get many honest-to-goodness Country and Western fans in this part of Manchester. I said so to my dad, trying to calm him down a bit.

'Guess you're right, Lou honey,' he admitted, adjusting his black stetson and pulling his fringed suede jacket tight round himself to keep out the cold. 'Ain't seen many Lonesome Cowboys in Didsbury village, no sirree.'

Dad is not a Lonesome Cowboy. He isn't even American. I suppose he could be lonesome, but the nearest he's ever been to a cow is a Tesco milk carton. He's just a person with a vivid imagination, and likes pretending he's in Nashville, Tennessee, strolling down to the Grand Old Opry, hobnobbing with George Jones and Merle Haggard and all the good ol' boys, and buying drinks for Tammy and Dolly and Nanci in saloon bars filled with fiddle music and people in checked shirts. He loves Country and Western music. We play it all the time on our ghetto-squeaker, ('Too small for a blaster,' says Dad), and I know all the songs by heart. He and my mother called me after Emmylou Harris ('The greatest of them all,' says Dad), but when I got to secondary school, I told them my name was Louise. My mother had been gone eight years by then, so I didn't see her coming up to the school and putting them straight.

Dad and I don't know where she is. She's never been back, never written to me, never sent a birthday card or a Christmas card.

'She lit out and disappeared,' my dad says wistfully, 'just like a woman in one of those Country songs.'

My mother leaving made my dad worse. He spent more and more of his time imagining and dreaming and pretending and listening to his tapes. Somewhere along the line, as he puts it, he became properly divorced. The jobs he got became more and more grotty, and so did the flats and bedsits we lived in. I used to hate the holidays. At least at school there were people to play with and hot dinners. In the holidays, I used to have to spend quite a lot of my time hanging about wherever Dad was working, because there was no one he could leave me with. Things are a bit better now. We live in this enormous dilapidated house with about eight other people. It's called a Communal House, which means we share the rent and take turns with the washing-up and the cooking. Dad has a tiny bedroom on his own, but I have to share with Sarah and Bryony who are OK but too little to be really interesting. They are also noisy. There's a big lounge for everyone, and a TV which sometimes works and sometimes doesn't. There's a video which is useless. It chews up films and makes them come out stripey, so we never watch it. I don't care. I read books all the time. I joined the library with Dad when we came to live here. I couldn't believe it at first. They let you have all these books to read, and you don't have to pay for them. When you've read one lot, you just go and get more. It's amazing. I read all the time. I love it. You can forget you're on a smelly second-hand sofa in Manchester. You can go anywhere you like.

I was slightly dreading Christmas, though, until Dad got the new job. We spent it here last year and it was awful. All the other people in our house had gone to their families, but my grandma and grandpa are dead, and Dad was an only child. We rattled round the chilly house. We had to unfreeze a chicken and cook it, and we didn't have crackers because just the two of us in funny paper hats would have looked pathetic. The TV was working, so we watched that a lot, and ate chocolate biscuits and listened to songs about Momma and Daddy and the fields back home and other stuff that made me want to cry. The worst thing of all about last Christmas was that Affleck's Palace, where my dad had a kind of half-job, was closed for four whole days over the holiday.

Affleck's is my favourite place in the world. I suppose if you look at it one way, it's nothing but a market on three floors of an old building that used to be a department store called Affleck and Brown. On each floor there are small booths and little stalls and bigger shop spaces, all pushed in together, as if someone not very tidy was in charge of a crowded dolls' house. But you won't find cheese or fruit pies or sheets of greenish tripe or pig's trotters in Affleck's. What you will find is second-hand clothes, silver jewellery, joss sticks, Doc Marten boots in every colour you can think of, velvet waistcoats, patchwork trousers, hand-painted T-shirts, amber beads the size of gobstoppers, crafts from Latin America and Africa, postcards, old records, Heavy Metal tapes, lace and chiffon scarves, hats made of velvet and a café where you can go and sit and sniff all the smells that are hanging around. It's always crowded at Affleck's.

Students roam around in packs and it's a good place to go when it's raining if you're homeless and hungry. It often is raining in Manchester, and I recognize the faces of some of the people I've seen begging at Piccadilly or in the Arndale Centre. Most people don't look at beggars, but I do. The young ones have grey faces and the old ones frighten me, because I can sometimes imagine my dad getting like them, singing his songs to the accompaniment of our ghetto-squeaker outside the Royal Exchange, with passers-by throwing change into a hat. His job at Affleck's isn't secure. Dad knows someone who makes these T-shirts, and he's helping him keep an eye on the stall for a few hours every day. That's all, and even though I can wander around for hours quite happily, the pay is dismal.

And then, this new job at Cedar House came up. Bill, the T-shirt man, told Dad about it.

'They're opening that Cedar House in Didsbury over Christmas,' he said. 'It's been done up nicely, and it's going to be a school sometime in the New Year, so they say, but just over Christmas, they're using it for the old folks. They need someone to do caretaking and odd jobs for a bit. Just while the old folks are there.'

'Where do these old people come from?' I asked my dad, on our way to the interview. 'It's not tramps, is it?'

'Oh no,' said Dad. 'It's just that some old folks' homes close at Christmas, because so many people go and visit their families, and the staff need a bit of a break as well. This lot that are coming to Cedar House, well, they've got no one at all and nowhere to go.'

I was going to the interview as well, because my dad had decided that Mrs Brightson, the person in charge of the school who was also running a Senior Citizens scheme at the house over Christmas, should see how clean and well-behaved I was, and what a help I would be around the place.

'Otherwise,' he'd said, 'she'll think the worst. If I say I've got a teenage daughter, she's going to imagine black leather and nose-rings, you betcha!'

We can't afford leather, and I'm frightened of nose-rings, or I suppose I might have turned out to be the kind of teenager Mrs Brightson might be scared of. As it happens, I'm small and my hair is long and fair, and I was wearing black jeans and my best jersey, a hand-knitted Fair Isle that I'd found in Humana for £3.

Mrs Brightson liked my dad. I could tell. He was being less cowboyish than usual and I think she was impressed that a single father should have coped so well with bringing up a daughter all on his own.

'She's a credit to you, Mr Edwards,' she said. 'And I expect she'll be willing to lend a hand over Christmas.'

I nodded demurely, and my dad got the job and said 'Yeehah!' and bought me this beautiful notebook. I've filled fifteen pages already. Tonight we are packing and tomorrow we'll be moving into Cedar House, going to that part of town where there are gardens and trees, and you never see homeless people with grey skin huddled in doorways, holding up bits of cardboard, asking for money.

Once upon a time long ago, Cedar House was a home for just one family. I can't think how they filled all the rooms. There are twenty bedrooms, arranged along corridors and up little staircases and around a kind of gallery. You can stand outside your bedroom and look down into the front hall below you. Even if there were fifteen children in the family, there would still be all the downstairs rooms to do things in. Cedar House had a ballroom, a drawing-room, a library, a music-room, a dining-room and a billiard-room. Mrs Brightson still called them by their long-ago names, though as far as I could see they were just plain old lounges filled with beige armchairs and sofas and a dining-room where the tables had orange plastic chairs all round them. The house was big and square and echoey on the inside, and the dozen old people who were staying over Christmas wandered through all the spaces, gathering near the gas fire in the drawing-room or round the colour TV in what used to be the library as if they were frightened of being anywhere on their own.

I was a little nervous of the old people at first. They seemed so wispy and small and wrinkled, and they walked so carefully everywhere, as if they were afraid of breaking into small pieces at the least bump. Lots of them had fingers that looked like tree-roots. It was hard to imagine them striding about or running or cooking, or doing anything athletic. That's what I thought at first, but then they started to talk to me. I was often sitting reading in the lounge when they drifted in feeling like a natter, and so I learned that Mrs Thomas was County Tennis Champion in her day, and Miss Ballantyne was a dancer once, and Mr Simpson ('You should really call me Sergeant Simpson') was a dashing soldier in the war and spent his time driving round the desert in a tank.

'I never realized,' I told him, 'that you all had such interesting lives.'

'What we've got,' he answered, nodding at me and poking the air with a gnarled finger, 'is Histories. We've got a Past, every last one of us, but not much of a Future, eh? Eh?' He thought this was a really good joke every time he said it, but I only really found it funny once.

As well as Mrs Brightson and Dad there were also two helpers who weren't exactly nurses or cleaning ladies, but something in between. Then there was Ruby, the cook. As soon as I saw her, I thought; maybe this is the one. I ought to explain. Ever since I was five, I've been on the look-out for a mother. I haven't told anyone. I especially haven't told my dad, because he's tried so hard to be a father and a mother to me that it would be rude, I think, to say that yes, I've been lying all these years, and yes, I do miss my mother, and yes, I envy other girls their mothers and that's why I try not to go to other people's houses too much. It makes me ache and that's the truth, so I try to avoid it. I'm not as bad now as I used to be. I've got accustomed to it over the years, and a lot of the time I don't think about it at all, but at this time of the year, it gets bad. Mothers come to carol concerts at school. Mothers make mince pies for the Gala and Jumble Sale. My friends are counting out their money and moaning 'I don't know what to get my mum, I don't honestly' till I feel I could scream. All the ads on TV feature exhausted mothers in aprons spooning gravy over gigantic turkeys, or smiling dewy-eyed at their poppets opening The Perfect Present. I can't bear it. I can't remember too much about my real mother. My dad kept some photos for my sake, but he's burned a lot as well. She smelled lovely, I remember that, and she seems to have been pretty and cheerful-looking. Not at all like a mother who runs away and leaves her husband and daughter. I used to think she went because of something I'd done, but my dad says no, it was just another man, like it is in the songs on our ghetto-squeaker. But why did she never get in touch, I wanted to know.

'Too painful for her, I expect,' Dad'd say. 'The thought of you must be making her feel guilty.'

She hated being unhappy, he used to tell me, and I'd nod, as though I understood and all the time part of me was saying, 'But what about me? I don't like being unhappy either. It's not fair.'

I gave up on my own mother long ago, but that doesn't stop me being on the look-out for a new, improved one. My dad has had some girlfriends, but not one of them has lasted long. He never says why, but I bet it's me. I think it's because they don't want me for a daughter, but I've never told my dad. He'd deny it. According to him, I'm the cat's pyjamas, and he doesn't see that other people don't feel quite the same.

Ruby, though, was perfect. She was good-looking in a comfortable, motherly way, with laughing blue eyes and a nice, cuddly sort of figure, and she never minded chatting, or letting me help her prepare the food. She seemed to be about the same age as my dad, as far as I could tell. Her work kept her in the kitchen a lot of the time, so she didn't come across my dad all that often, but I'd worked out that that might be an advantage. She could meet me first and get to like me ever such a lot, so that when she got to know Dad properly, she'd fall into his arms with a sigh and we'd all live happily ever after.

I tried hard to find out whether Ruby had a husband or not, without much success. For someone who was as talkative as she was, there wasn't much about herself she gave away. I kept opening my mouth to ask whether she had any children, and then closing it again – I don't know why.

'What're you getting for Christmas, then?' she said to me one day.

I said, 'I haven't bought it yet, so I don't know.'

Ruby was chopping vegetables, but she stopped in mid-chop, and looked at me.

I said hurriedly, 'My dad says he never knows what I want, and it's pointless wasting money on something I'll not be that chuffed with. So I choose it. And I have to choose his present from me as well. Socks, it is, usually. Sometimes I can find something a bit different.'

Ruby shook her head, without comment, and I changed the subject, making a note to ask Dad for some money tonight. Christmas will soon be here.

I bought my present earlier today, and it's the most beautiful thing I've ever had. I can't wait till Christmas morning, when I unwrap it. It's lucky Dad has taken charge of it, or I'd be looking at it every few minutes, stroking it and sniffing at it. I can't get over how lucky I was to have found it. At one point I thought I wouldn't have anything.

I set out for town first thing this morning feeling like a millionaire. I had three five-pound notes in my purse.

'That's ten pounds on you, and five on me, and don't try and cheat or I'll know,' my dad had said.

I hate Christmas shopping. There are too many people pushing and shoving along the pavements, too many tinny carols being churned out at top volume in every shop, and too much decoration, and glittery red and green, and stupid-looking Father Christmases with cottonwool beards half coming off. The least tinselly place I could think of was Affleck's Palace, so I went there. I knew a lot of the stall holders, and in 'Silver Bells and Cockle Shells' there were rings for ten pounds and under that I liked the look of.

As I got off the bus at Piccadilly, a thin, sleety rain began to fall out of a sky like a grey blanket. I turned up the collar on my coat and wished I had a scarf or a hat. I thought, why does it never snow properly here? It's not fair. The white flakes should float down and cover up all the litter on the black pavements and then we would all tread on it as if it were a soft white carpet. Instead of which, all we get is needlepricks of icy sleet and a wind that could slice strips off a person's face. I walked past Lewis's and crossed the road over to Debenham's, and then I saw them: a thin young girl and a dog. The girl was wearing jeans and a skimpy denim jacket. She had cropped hair and fingerless gloves and a face like a ghost. The dog was black and so skinny you could see his ribs. This girl wasn't even bothering to hold a sign up. She had squashed herself and her dog into a kind of alcove just past the optician's shop. My heart started thumping. I had all that money . . . it wasn't right for me to have all that money and for her to have nothing. The dog looked at me and made a whimpering noise in his throat. I took one of the fivers out of my purse and went up to her.

'Merry Christmas,' I said. She didn't look much older than me. She smiled, then frowned.

'Are you sure?' she whispered. 'It's a lot of money.'

'Yes, I'm sure,' I answered. 'I've got enough. Truly.'

Then she said a funny thing. I remember it because it's not the sort of thing you expect someone to say to you at eleven o'clock in the morning in the middle of a crowded city street. It was more what you'd expect to hear in church. She looked at me with very clear, grey eyes and laid a pale hand like a claw on my sleeve.

'I know,' she said, 'that you will reap your reward.'

After I'd left the girl and her dog behind, I felt good for a few minutes. I was a kind and generous person. I had made someone a bit happier, and that made me happier until I realized that now I only had ten pounds for me and my dad. I sighed. Bang goes my ring, I thought, unless I can find something really cheap for Dad. I felt bad the moment this thought came into my head, and I walked round Affleck's feeling guilty for a bit, not even looking properly at anything, just glancing about. Dad's present, it seems to me now, looking back, practically jumped up and waved itself under my nose shouting, 'Buy me! Buy me for your father! I'm just what he wants.'

I was looking at a tray of rings in 'Silver Bells' and beginning to feel downhearted because there was nothing I liked and could also afford. Out of the corner of my eye, I caught sight of something. I could see turquoise, flashing silver, and I turned round to look properly.

'New stock,' said Marymary, the owner of the stall. 'Western-style ties.'

I knew at once that Dad would love a leather thong that fastened at the neck with a turquoise and silver clasp. I looked at the price tag. £6.99. I bought one without a second thought. There were now three pound coins and one penny left for me, and it was all my doing. If I had a grotty Christmas present this year, I had no one to blame but myself.

'You look,' said a voice from behind me, 'as if you'd lost a shilling and found sixpence, as we used to say in the days of the Old Money.'

I turned to see who had spoken to me, and there behind me was a stall I had never seen before. The name 'Burning Memories' was painted on a sign hanging on the front of the counter, and the stall was about the size of three phone booths squashed together. The walls were hung with purple velvet and on every flat surface there were candles.

I said, 'I've never seen so many candles before! Have you only just opened?'

The lady behind the counter considered this. In the end she smiled and said only, 'Here today, gone tomorrow.'

She was peculiar, even by the standards of Affleck's Palace. I couldn't decide how old she was. Her hair was grey, but she wore it curling over her shoulders, like a young girl. Her arms were covered with bracelets from the wrist to the elbow: gold snakes biting their own tails, copper bangles, and amber ones and some made of painted wood. Her clothes seemed to have neither a beginning nor an end. She was covered in layers of fabric that slid over her, and clung and floated and draped themselves around her body. She had bad teeth and hardly any wrinkles, and her eyes were clear and yellow, like a black cat's eyes. I shivered a little. This person was weird.

'What's your name?' she asked gently, as if she sensed that I felt a little frightened.

'Emmylou Edwards,' I said, and added, 'I love your candles. I didn't realize you could have so many different kinds and colours.'

'Delighted to meet you, Emmylou. My name is

Clio, and yes, there are as many different candles as there are . . .' she looked around, searching for the right words, 'dreams and desires in the heart, or memories in the mind. For every hope in your breast, I have a candle that will burn to make it come true. There are candles to make you forget, candles that can light a spark of love where no love is . . . oh, they have powers you could never imagine! There are shapes and colours to suit every occasion. I make them all by hand. Come in and have a proper look around.'

She moved aside and I slid in behind the counter. I thought, it's like a proper cave, and I was surprised that there was enough space for me and Clio to walk about in.

'It's bigger than it looks,' I said.

'Most things are not what they seem,' said Clio. 'As you will discover.'

'And there's so much . . . so much to look at.'

As well as the candles, there were small bottles containing oils that looked like jewels melted down. There were crystals in a basket, blazing where the light touched them, and another basket full of marble eggs that were heavy and smooth to the touch. Perhaps, I thought, I should buy one of those. They were only £1.99. I had almost decided on a pink one, when I saw the candle and knew that it was mine with a certainty that seems stupid looking back. What if it had been too expensive? If I say the candle was green, that won't begin to describe what it looked like. It was a swirling mass made of every green in the world (seas, forests, leaves, grass, emeralds, jade, lime), moulded into a shape that was almost but not quite round. The surface of the candle had been carved into patterns that looked like plants or leaves or curling waves or small dragons. It was hard to work out what they were, but they twisted and crept all over the candle like living, growing things.

'I like that one,' I said, pointing up to it, 'but I expect it's too expensive. I haven't got much money left.'

'This one,' said Clio, 'is very special. It's one of my scented range. Have a sniff.'

She set the candle down in front of me. I bent my head to fill my nostrils with its fragrance, and it smelled of my mother. I had to have it.

I said, 'It smells exactly like my mother, and I haven't seen her since I was very small.'

Clio smiled. 'It smells of the past,' she said. 'Wait till you light it.'

'I'll never light it,' I said. 'I never want it to burn away.'

'You must light it on Christmas Day,' said Clio. 'If you do not promise to light it then, I will not sell it to you. I shall raise the price so that you can't afford it, unless you promise me.'

I sighed. Perhaps I should have the pink egg after all. At least I would still own it in January. Did I want a candle that would just disappear? Wasn't that a real waste of money? I don't know what happened to my common sense. Instead of saying, no, I don't want it after all, I said, 'OK. I promise. How much is it?'

'It's three pounds and a penny,' said Clio. 'By coincidence.'

I stared at her. How did she know what was in my purse? The yellow eyes shone at me like lanterns, and I shivered. X-ray eyes, I thought, as if I were in a science fiction movie. I shook my head to clear it of stupid thoughts, and then I emptied my purse out on to the counter.

'Have you got your bus-fare home?' Clio asked.

'Oh yes,' I said. 'That's separate. That's not Christmas money.'

'Good,' Clio said. 'Now I shall wrap your candle for you.'

She found some sheets of purple tissue paper and folded my beautiful present into them. The silence grew between us, so I said, just to make conversation, 'I like the name of your shop. There's a song called *Burning Memories*. Waylon Jennings sings it. Do you know his songs?'

Clio shook her head. 'I've heard neither of him nor of his song. Is it a sad one?'

'It's about this man, burning letters and photographs and things, burning everything that reminds him of his wife. She's left him, you see.'

'A very sad song then.' She smiled. 'There you are. I've managed to find a carrier bag, which doesn't often happen. Don't forget your promise.'

On the way back to the bus stop, the thought of the candle in its tissue paper wrapping made me feel warm inside. The girl and her dog had gone from the alcove beside the opticians. Perhaps they were having a lovely meal somewhere in a café full of warm light and good food. The candle in its carrier bag swung from my hand as I walked. Maybe this was what the girl meant. Maybe the candle was my reward, I thought. Oh, I wish it was Christmas Day tomorrow. I wish the time would fly.

Christmas Day is over. It's Boxing Day, which I always think of as a flat, featureless sort of day: like a Sunday, but worse. My candle is nothing but a hard puddle of green wax on a saucer, but it was worth it. We had, we all had, a magical time, a time that's busy disappearing from my mind already. I have to write down what happened before I forget it. If anyone else reads this, they probably wouldn't believe me. They'd most likely say: it's quite understandable at Christmas. I haven't spoken to anyone about what happened. I'm only sure of one thing: my candle made it happen. Whatever sort of thing went on, Clio knew about it. I know the candle was responsible, because until I lit it, everything had been normal.

Dad and I opened our presents early in the morning. The tie made him shout 'Yee-hah!' as I had known it would, and he put it on with his pyjamas. He was a bit perplexed by my candle, but said in the end, 'Well, if that's what you wanted . . .' and wandered off to shave and dress and get ready for breakfast.

We all ate together in the dining-room every day, and when I reached my place, there was a small pile of presents waiting there for me. I was so embarrassed, I didn't know where to look.

'Open your presents, dear,' said Miss Ballantyne,

and I blushed scarlet and started tearing paper off my parcels. Everything was quite small: soap and chocolates and lacy hankies, but I felt as though I'd been given the most wonderful things in the world. Ruby had given me a £5 book token.

'Because you're always reading,' she explained, and I was so pleased, I went over to where she was helping one of the old gentlemen to cut up his bacon, and gave her a big hug.

'Thank you,' I said to them all. 'I feel awful. I haven't got anyone a present, and I'm really sorry.'

There were cries of how it didn't matter, and that Christmas was for the kiddies, really, wasn't it?

Then I said, 'But I'll share one of my presents with you at dinner time. It'll make everything really special.'

I didn't realize when I said that quite how special it would turn out to be.

After breakfast, I went to help Ruby with all the last-minute things in the kitchen. She had a glass of sherry next to her on the working surface, otherwise I don't think she would have said anything. What she did say was, 'My daughter would be just a little bit older than you are . . .' Then she laughed. 'I think of her most at this time of year. It's true, isn't it, what they were all saying? Christmas *is* for the kiddies. Most of the time I'm fine.' Tears were pouring down her cheeks now. 'Give us a tissue, Lou dear, and let's say no more about it. I expect it's the drink talking.'

'Is she dead?' I asked. 'Your daughter?'

'She might just as well be. I haven't seen her since she was a week old.'

I must have looked puzzled, because Ruby went on, 'I gave her up for adoption. Everyone (the doctor, my parents, even me, quite often) thought it was for the best. The father ... he was long gone. A lot of people told me it was the right thing to do, and I believed them. Give her a better chance in life, they said.' She took another sip from the glass of sherry. 'They were wrong, though, weren't they? I miss her, even after all these years. It wasn't so bad while Mike, my husband, was alive. I used to hope we might have children of our own, but now he's gone ... well, it's too late, of course.'

'You could marry again,' I suggested, thinking of my father. 'You could become somebody's step-mother.' Ruby said nothing, so I plunged on. I'd never get such a good chance to talk again. I said, 'I wouldn't mind you being my stepmother. In fact, I'd like it.'

Ruby laughed and hugged me and called me a proper caution.

I said, rather huffily, 'I don't see what's so funny. My dad's dead nice. He looks quite young for his age.'

'He's very nice,' said Ruby, 'and a very good dad to you, I can see that, but ... he's not my type, love, that's all. What is it you young people say? I don't fancy him.' She went bright red and added, 'I don't know what's got into me today. I don't honestly. It's all this sherry so early in the day.'

Ruby changed the subject then, but I'd already made my mind up. As soon as Affleck's opened after

Christmas, I'd go back to Clio's shop and buy some kind of love potion. I knew, I just knew she would have one that would work a miracle. I cut into another Brussels sprout, and smiled to myself.

Christmas dinner was a very jolly meal. We all ate too much, and then I lit the candle, which I'd put ready on a saucer beside my plate. As the flame grew brighter, a thread of pale green smoke rose from the wick and curled up into the afternoon air. Up and up it went and you could see it clearly. It wasn't dispersing. It was making shapes up near the ceiling, like a ribbon of mist. I felt Time stretching out all around me. No one at the table said a word.

'If I don't close my eyes,' said one of the old ladies, a Mrs Rosebery, 'I shall fall asleep right here at the table.'

'I know exactly how you feel,' said Ruby.

'I could do with a spot of shut-eye myself,' said my dad.

Before I knew where I was, I was sitting all alone in the dining-room with the debris of our Christmas dinner in front of me on the table. Outside the window, it was already dark. My candle was the only light, and that was odd. Had someone switched off the electric light on the way to their afternoon nap? I pushed my chair aside, and picked up the saucer with my candle on it. I turned away from the table towards the window, and saw that the whole room was different. What had happened to the cheerful striped cotton curtains that were there a moment ago? Now, velvet drapes hung at the window, and I could just make out, in the yellow candlelight, a crystal chandelier above my head. And the table with all the remains of our Christmas dinner – where was that? There was something very strange going on. I remember thinking, I'll find the others, then everything will be normal. I left the dining-room, carrying the candle and went upstairs.

I don't know how to describe what I found there. I went from bedroom to bedroom, knocking on the door of each one. No one ever told me to come in, but I opened each bedroom door as I went past, and found (I don't know how to put it better than this) a scene from the past. I could tell it was that because everyone looked so young. I know they were real scenes that I saw, real memories brought to life, because when I went into my dad's room, there he was with me on his knee. I looked about two years old, and I was waving my new doll about by the leg. My pretty mother was smiling at me and blowing me kisses. I've still got that doll, only she's much older now. We were in our old house. I would have said I didn't remember it at all, but I recognized the patterns in the carpet, and there on the chest-of-drawers was the album cover of one of our oldest albums, *Elite Hotel* by Emmylou Harris, my namesake. There was even a Christmas tree in the corner, hung with coloured balls and stars and small foil-wrapped chocolates. My dad looked happier than I'd ever seen him. I stared and stared at this scene, taking note of every single detail, so that I'd remember it to write down later, and here I am writing it down and already it's a bit hazy, like something I may have dreamed. But I didn't dream it. I walked with my green candle from room to room, and in every one, someone was happy – happier than they'd ever been. Mrs Thomas was handing out plates of food to her children, those very same children, probably, who had arranged for her to stay at Cedar House this year.

Other old people, made miraculously younger, were dancing, carol-singing, decorating rooms I'd never seen before. Ruby, a very young Ruby, was helping her sisters make mince-pies late at night. The kitchen clock said two o'clock. They were singing and giggling as they worked. I couldn't bear to see how happy she looked, how much sadder she had looked this morning. I went to my room and watched the candle, what was left of it, burn down to a pool of green wax. As I lay down on my bed, I thought: it's like seeing everybody's dearest memories ... like holiday snapshots come to life, everyone's happiest Christmas, the loveliest pieces of the past, brought back for a while. I closed my eyes and slept.

I wasn't going to mention my candle, but a few days later my dad said, 'I don't know what Ruby put into the Christmas pudding but I had the best dream ever that afternoon. I can't really bring it to mind now, but I know it was wonderful. You were tiny, that I can remember. Wow! I loved that dream.'

'That wasn't Ruby's pudding. It was my candle. The smoke from my candle put everyone to sleep.'

'Maybe they all had wonderful dreams too, you

never know,' he said, and disappeared before I could tell him that they did.

There's good news and there's bad news. The good news is, Mrs Brightson is so impressed with Dad that she's asked him to be the caretaker for the school that's going to open here in April. I shall have to change schools to one that's nearer Cedar House, but I don't mind. I'm used to it. When I was little, we moved all the time. Now that my dad has got a proper job, he might settle down.

The bad news is Ruby left before I could get to Affleck's Palace. She would have done just fine for my mother, if I'd had a little help from Clio. I mentioned it to my dad, and he laughed.

'I liked her well enough, Lou honey, but she didn't make my heart beat faster, and that's a fact.'

As Dad spoke, a pleasant thought occurred to me.

'Is Cedar House going to be a girls' school?' I asked.

'Yes,' said Dad. 'Girls only, aged five to eleven. A preparatory school, Mrs Brightson called it. Very exclusive and expensive.'

A very exclusive and expensive school would have lots of teachers. Maybe one of them would fall in love with my dad. I don't expect exclusive and expensive teachers notice caretakers very often, so I shall definitely need some help from Clio. Tomorrow, I thought, I shall go and ask her advice.

I went to Affleck's this morning. It was pouring with

rain as I got off the bus and I was drenched by the time I got there. No one I asked had ever heard of Clio, and 'Burning Memories' was nowhere to be found.

I felt sad all the way back to the bus stop, but then I caught sight of the girl, the one I'd given a fiver to. She and her skinny black dog disappeared into Back George Street, and at once I felt happier, though I wasn't sure why. Maybe, I thought, Dad'll manage to fall in love all by himself without any help from a magic potion, and if he doesn't, well, we can manage on our own. The sun broke through the clouds as I got on to the bus and flashed and sparkled on every single puddle between Piccadilly and Cedar House.

# Miranda's Child

Sometimes, while I'm waiting for Annie to come out of playgroup, I pretend I'm her mother. I'm too old for pretend games at sixteen, I know, but I've always played them, as long as I can remember, and I don't know how to stop myself.

Of course, I'm not her mother, I'm her nanny. I've always wanted to be a nanny. That's why I left school in the summer, in spite of spindly Mrs Waister, the careers teacher, giving me a good old glare over the top of her glasses which seem to have settled forever in a groove halfway down her nose. I'd made up my mind, and what's more, I'd even convinced my parents that I'd start proper nanny training when I was seventeen. I'd applied for a course which started next year.

'But what'll you do till then?' my mum wanted to know. 'You can't hang about the house all day.'

'I shall get a job,' I announced and I did get one,

almost straightaway, so ya boo and sucks to the lot of them: everyone who kept rabbiting on at me about youth unemployment, recessions, dole queues, etc. My friend Pam was quite impressed when I told her I'd landed if not the job of my dreams, then something almost as good.

'How did you do it?' she asked.

'I just wrote out a card saying what I'd like to be able to do, and Mrs Jarrett phoned up after it had been in the newsagent's for two days.'

'I wouldn't know what to say,' Pam said. 'What did you put?'

'I put: "Sixteen-year-old school leaver waiting to train as nanny would like to help out looking after small child. No experience, but willing to learn and very friendly and affectionate. Reasonable rates." Then I put my 'phone number.'

'You've landed in the jam,' Pam said. 'Rowena Jarrett is mega-famous and all you've got to do is pick her kid up from playgroup and keep her happy till four o'clock. And there's the housekeeper always around to help out in an emergency. It's what I call a cushy job, me.'

I couldn't deny it. The Jarretts live on Elm Road in one of those huge houses you look at while you're on your way to somewhere else. I'd never been anywhere so posh in my life before, and at the beginning I was a bit nervous about it, but I don't notice it so much now I'm used to it, and the Jarretts are ever so nice. They're both presenters on Granada TV, and are hardly ever about. Freda the housekeeper ('Not a bit like Mrs Danvers in *Rebecca*,' I told Pam) is a chatty soul with a family life which is, to use her own words, 'as good as anything you'll see on *Coronation Street*'. And as for Annie, well, she's lovely. She's thin and dark and clever and always talking and moving and wanting stories and more games and I love her to bits.

'She sounds exhausting,' said Pam.

'She is,' I said, 'but it's great. I love going to playgroup to meet her every day.'

That's the best part of this job. That's when I play my best pretend-game of all, imagining that I'm a real mother and that Annie is my real child. I've always longed to have a baby and one day I will. Last year, I went to see my cousin Sheila's baby at St Mary's, just after he was born. I stood there staring at him for ages. I couldn't get used to how small and soft he was, how easily he could be hurt. It seemed amazing that so many babies survived, when they were so frail.

'Don't you believe it,' said Sheila. 'Quite tough, they are, in some ways. Well, they have to be, don't they?' She didn't say why, and started talking about something else, but I couldn't stop thinking about what it must be like, carrying a child for all those months and then losing it in the end.

'That girl,' Sheila whispered, inclining her head towards a corner of the room, 'I don't think there's any dad to speak of there . . . not so's you'd notice. Dead sad, I call it, at her age. Still, it's a lovely baby . . . I don't know. I feel sorry for her, I do truly.'

I agreed with Sheila, but there was still a bit of me

that felt envious. That's why I like this game, outside playgroup. All the real mothers realize I'm only a mother's help, because they all know that Annie is Rowena Jarrett's daughter, and Rowena is a Local Celebrity, so there's no harm done. Also, because Rowena is who she is, lots of the mums come over and talk to me and I've got to know some of them quite well. The ones I don't speak to I just look at. There are all sorts outside that playgroup: lots wearing cagoules and woolly hats, a few in suits with briefcases, one rather vulgar one in fake-fur leopard skin and three-inch heels, and loads of gold-coloured jewellery, and of course there are lots of au pairs from Spain or Sweden or Germany. And last term . . . last term there was Miranda.

I named her Miranda. I never found out what her name was. She was different. I knew it from the very first time I saw her, waiting under the laburnum tree, some way away from the other mothers. She had ash-blonde hair and a face that was so pale it was almost transparent. She always stood in the shade. So pale . . . perhaps the sunlight actually hurt her skin, and she avoided it. I knew there were people who suffered like that. Her hands were pale too, and fragile-looking against the black fabric of her coat. From time to time she would push her hair back with her fingers, and they hovered near her face like wounded birds. I looked at her, and tried to imagine a story for her, some kind of setting, some life, but it was just as if there were a wall of glass all around her that not only kept people from talking to her, but that also deflected

119

any curious thoughts or questions that other people sent out to her. I wondered and wondered about her, but she defeated my imagination. All I did know was this: she was different, and what made her different was the quality of her waiting.

I came to this conclusion after I'd been watching her for about a week. I should explain what I mean. I'd noticed that all the mothers outside the church hall where the playgroup was held had their own special ways of waiting and of meeting their kids. Some were a bit anxious. I could see them craning their necks as soon as the doors were opened, trying to see inside the room, to check that their darling was still there and hadn't come to any harm during the morning. Some mothers were fusspots, and didn't even bother saying hello before they started tutting over unfastened coat buttons, and pulling on discarded gloves. Some were always in a hurry to leave, and pulled their offspring down the road like the Red Queen did to Alice: faster, faster.

Miranda simply stood under the laburnum tree and stared. Across the gravel from the tree to the door of the church hall it was almost possible to see, like thin wires, the lines of longing, the waves of wanting that drew her eyes to the spot where soon her child would appear. Day after day I watched her waiting, and day after day I made up my mind to stay behind and see which one was her kid, how they met, where they went, what they were like together. It never seemed to work out like that. Annie would come bounding out, restless after having sat quietly on a bench for the last ten minutes, and want to be gone, to be home, to be off, racing down the road with me after her. I never managed, at first, to spot Miranda's child. And then, one day, I saw her. Annie was dawdling, picking her way, tightrope-walker fashion, along the edge of the pavement. I walked along beside her, holding her hand. Every few seconds I turned to look back at the laburnum tree and at last, there she was: a pretty girl with red-gold hair, wearing a padded raincoat in a light shade of blue. She wore long white socks and shiny patent-leather shoes with a strap across the instep.

I noticed her shoes particularly. Most of the children at playgroup wore trainers. These black shoes seemed old-fashioned, formal and out of place. The child ran straight to Miranda, under the tree. A pretty girl with long red hair . . . Annie asked me something, just at that moment, and when I turned to look for Miranda and her child again they were gone. But I'd seen her.

After that, I saw her quite often, running to her mother, usually after the other children had left. I never saw Miranda hugging her daughter, or talking to her in any way, and this I found difficult to understand. All the time she was waiting, Miranda was clearly longing for her. Why, then, had I never seen her give the child as much as a pat on the head?

The mothers talked about Miranda among themselves. Gossiped. Speculated. Nobody spoke to her properly, although a few brave souls ventured an occasional 'Good morning' or 'Lovely day!' When I told Pam about her, she said she was probably a one-parent family from Oakhill Flats.

One Saturday, we saw her sitting on a bench outside Didsbury Library.

'That's her,' I whispered. 'That's Miranda.'

'She's quite pretty,' Pam whispered back, 'but dead white. Should try a bit of blusher. You tell her.'

'Oh, yeah,' I said. 'Great idea. Me going up to this person I've never even said "hello" to and just coming out with: "Me and my mate Pam reckon you could do with a bit more blusher!"'

'Well,' said Pam, 'you'd have to be slightly more tactful than that.'

'I don't think she can have much money, though,' I said. 'Her kid is always in that same old blue raincoat.'

'Is it dirty?'

I thought about Miranda's child.

'No,' I said. 'It looks brand new. She never has a speck of dirt on her. It's funny. I never thought of that before.'

A few days after seeing Miranda in Didsbury, it was half-term and I forgot all about her. On the first day back, though, there she was again, under the tree. I began, simply because she was so unchanging, to lose interest in her. I stopped, most days, looking out for her daughter.

Once, I asked Annie, 'Do you ever play with a little girl with red hair?'

'No,' said Annie.

'Do you know who I mean? The little girl with the red hair and the shiny black shoes?'

122

'Yes,' said Annie, but she sounded very hesitant. You should never show kids by your tone of voice what you want them to say. Nine times out of ten, they'll say what you want, just to shut you up. I sighed, and decided Miranda's child and Annie weren't friends, but I knew she was there. Didn't I see her running across the gravel, almost every day? Didn't I turn to look at them under the tree as we walked down the road: red hair and gold hair under the black branches? Of course I did.

Then, one day, the child didn't come out of play-group. I was waiting for Annie after all the others had gone, because she had been specially chosen to stay behind and arrange the skeletons and pumpkins daintily for Miss Warner, ready for the Hallowe'en party the next day. The walls of the church hall were already covered with sugar-paper cut-outs of spiders, cauldrons, bats, witches and all the other creepy props Miss Warner could think of.

I was there, and Miranda was there, standing alone. Every leaf had gone from the branches of the laburnum tree by now and a drizzly rain was falling. I felt I had to speak to her. The silence hummed between us, filled my ears and deafened me. I had to say something, so I turned to the Great British Standby: the Weather.

'Awful, isn't it?' I said. 'This rain. Why don't we wait for them in the porch?'

She walked slowly from the tree to where I was standing, hiding from the weather. I glanced at her as she stood beside me, saying nothing, and at first I

123

thought her face was streaked with rain, but then I looked more closely and I could see that she was crying. My first instinct was to turn and run, because you don't expect to see an adult weeping in broad daylight, do you? I didn't know how to deal with it, but I didn't run away.

I said, 'What's the matter? Can I help? Is it your little girl?' (What made me say that? I don't know.)

She said, 'I haven't got a little girl.'

'But . . .' (Had I got it all wrong? Was she an au pair? An aunt? Childminder? Friend?) 'Then who is it that you pick up each day? The red-headed child in the blue raincoat?'

'Have you seen her?' Miranda whispered.

'Of course I've seen her.'

'And she has red hair?'

'That's right. Lovely and long.'

'I'm so glad . . .' Miranda burst into tears again, put her pale hands over her face and shook with sobs.

'But . . .' I was at a loss for words. 'You speak as though you can't see her. You speak as though you were blind.'

'I've never seen her,' Miranda said. 'I just imagine her, that's all. I imagine her all the time. Every single detail: shiny shoes with ankle straps . . . white socks.'

I nodded.

'Have you seen those?' she asked. 'I imagined them. I've pictured every single thing about her so strongly, every day. Every day since the day she was born. The day she was born and the day she died. She lived a few hours, that's all. Such a tiny life. Did you really see her?'

'Yes,' I said. There were a million things I wanted to know, to ask Miranda, to say, but nothing would come out of my mouth. It seemed to me that the whole of my known world was tilting dangerously around my head.

Miranda said, 'I'm so glad ... so happy you saw her. I don't have to wait here any more.'

She stepped out of the porch and walked away into the rain. She didn't look back once, not at me, not at the church hall. I stood watching the dripping branches of the laburnum tree, understanding suddenly why it was that I had never seen Miranda hugging her child, the child she loved so much. I understood also why she no longer needed to wait, to watch the door. I had confirmed something she'd only been able to imagine. I had given her thoughts a reality. I had seen her child for her. Her faith, her longing, had been vindicated.

I still don't understand why she never could see her little girl for herself. It seemed unfair, after imagining her so hard; hard enough for me to pick up what she was thinking and actually see it. I can't pretend I know how it happened. Perhaps my head is like a kind of receiver for other people's thoughts. This frightens me.

I never saw Miranda again, nor her child, though I think about them a lot.

I don't think I'll tell this story to anyone else.

# The Interview

Madame Vilenska thinks: they are all children and they understand nothing, nothing at all about what I am doing here. I am trying to create happiness and beauty in a world where little enough of it exists. Is that so wrong? Then tell me, someone, why I have been sitting here all day talking to one child after another, trying to find the one, the one who will comprehend me? I will press this buzzer . . . so . . . and yes, here is another one. Dark. Plain, but with possibilities . . . but then hasn't everyone the possibility of beauty? Isn't that the philosophy on which I have based my entire professional life? If not beauty, then glamour, chic, style, something. We can all change . . . oh, the bliss of metamorphosis . . . ducklings into swans.

Madame Vilenska says, 'Good morning, child. I'm so sorry to keep you waiting. Your name?'

'Pamela Duncan. My friends call me Pam.'

'And how old are you, Pam?' Madame Vilenska says the name, rolling it around in her mouth as though it were a plum stone, as though she is secretly looking for a place to spit it out.

'I'm seventeen.'

'And why have you applied for this job?'

'I've always wanted to be a hairdresser . . . ever since I was about six.'

Pam remembers a bus ride long ago. She and her mother on their way to town during the rush hour. They are stuck in a traffic jam, but she doesn't care. There is a row of boarded-up shops visible from the window. All the space is covered with posters. Pam has just learned to read and here is a patchwork quilt of words spread out in front of her, waiting to be said aloud. There are red and yellow and black words, printed in fat letters, or skinny ones, or uneven ones falling about all over the place. Normally such an abundance would keep Pam happily deciphering for long minutes, but then she notices something else: a line of tall, silver words right across the front of one of the closed-down shops.

Pam reads them aloud to her mother, '"Carroll Arden. Stylist to the Stars"  What does that mean?'

Pam's mother says, 'That used to be a hairdresser's long ago. That's what stylist means. Hairdresser.'

'But why stars?' Pam wants to know.

'Stars means actresses or dancers. There were lots of theatres and music halls round here in the old days. I shouldn't think Carroll Arden did film stars . . . there can't have been too many of those . . .'

Pam tastes the words, thinks of them for a long time. Stylist to the stars . . . it sounds beautiful to her still. Of course, these days, she knows exactly what stars are, but even so, when she says it to herself, an image of dark skies and whirling galaxies, of a million glittering silver pinpricks on a background like blue velvet comes into her mind.

'And what makes you think you have any talent in this area?' Madame Vilenska is suddenly fascinated, it seems, by her own hands. She stretches them out on the desk in front of her and appears to scrutinize them carefully: long, white fingers ending in glossy claws of nails painted the colour of aubergines. Madame Vilenska wears fingerless black lace gloves. She thinks, it is as though a black, scaly bark were growing over my skin . . . as though I were turning into a tree. She shivers. Better to turn into a tree than have to look at the brown stains spreading themselves over the backs of my hands . . . age . . . there is nothing that anyone can do about it. I try. No one tries harder than I do.

'I've always cut my mother's hair. And my sister's. All my friends get me to do their hair . . . you know . . . if there's a party, or anywhere special they have to go.'

'But there is more to this business than simply doing people's hair, is there not? Tell me five things . . . yes, five . . . that you think a hairdresser should try to achieve.'

Pam thinks, no one said there would be questions like this. She's a strange person, this Madame Vilenska. I can't decide whether she's beautiful or hideous.

Perhaps she's both at the same time . . . *can* you be both at the same time? Her lips are too shiny. Her hair . . . her hair looks like black patent leather . . . tightly wound into a bun at the back of her neck . . . it must pull so on her forehead. And her hands . . . I like the fingerless gloves. Would they look good on me? Or stupid?

'Well,' Pam frowns.

'Never frown,' says Madame Vilenska. 'I do not permit frowning. Frowning makes wrinkles and I do not like wrinkles, therefore I do not allow frowning. Is that clear?'

'Yes, Madame.' Silly old bag, Pam thinks, you're not my boss yet, are you? You can't tell me what to do with my face . . . 'Five things . . . well, first, I suppose, you have to give the customer what she asked for; secondly, you have to make her look good; thirdly, you mustn't hurt her . . . with scissors or hot water or anything . . . and you must smile and make her feel you like her . . . I can't really think of anything else . . .'

Pam's voice fades to silence.

'You are nearly right, but let me instruct you further. Most people, I have found, come here looking for two things: change and happiness. Women come here because they think that I can make them beautiful. They come because they are dissatisfied . . . with their hair, their skin . . . with their lives . . . with themselves. I offer them hope. Hope of beauty and happiness. I offer them transformations and metamorphoses . . . the possibility of love . . . a glimpse of paradise.'

Pam thinks, but the prices you ask! I saw them, up

on the wall in the black and silver reception area . . . a glimpse of paradise for those with the right sort of income. What about ordinary women? What about my mum and my teachers, and the women I see every day on the buses, in the supermarket, in the street? No meta-what's-it for them.

'I don't think,' says Pam, 'that most people come to the hairdresser's for happiness. Not really. I think they just want to make the best of themselves.'

'That,' says Madame Vilenska, 'is because you are young and innocent. But you will learn. Let me ask you something else now. What do you think are the reasons for human unhappiness?'

'Poverty, disease, war, famine, pain . . . unemployment . . .'

'True, all very true . . . in a cosmic sense. But you . . . tell me about yourself. Are you unhappy about anything?'

'Not at the moment . . . no. I'm OK on the whole. Now.'

'Have you ever been unhappy? You are clearly a girl who has led a sheltered life . . . but surely there must be something.'

'Well . . .'

'Don't be shy . . . tell me.'

Pam thinks, her eyes are like a lizard's eyes: flat and black and I can't see where the iris ends and the pupil begins. Maybe she's hypnotizing me . . . some people can do that, I know they can. I don't see why I should tell her everything. It's private . . . but if I don't, she might . . . I'll tell her a bit.

'There was this boy that I was going out with.'

'Yes . . . and did you love him?'

'Yes. People say you can't love anyone when you're fifteen . . .'

'Then they,' says Madame Vilenska with the nearest thing to a smile Pam has yet seen, 'have never been fifteen.'

Madame Vilenska thinks, fifteen is so long ago. I find it hard now to remember. I have used my own treatments too well. All that's left to me is scraps: pale green trees . . . and was there someone with dark brown eyes? I have a mauve blouse on . . . it's hard . . . so long ago . . . but still, there's something left there. A fluttering like a small bird trying out its wings . . . what rubbish. All that is long gone. Gone with everything else.

Madame Vilenska says, 'Tell me about it. Go on.'

Pam says, 'There's nothing much to tell. He was a boy I met. At a party. We went out together for a bit and then I found out he was seeing someone else as well, and I asked him about it. He said it was true. He . . . he liked this other girl better than me and so we broke up.' Pam looks at Madame Vilenska. 'It isn't anything unusual. It happens all the time. It happens to everyone.'

'Out of the mouths of babes and sucklings . . .' says Madame Vilenska. 'It most certainly does happen to everyone. And did it cause you suffering? Pain?'

'Yes, of course.'

'And do the memories cause you suffering, too? The memories of that time?'

'I try not to think about it too much. I think about something else most of the time.'

'But when you remember it, it hurts. Is that right?'

'Yes, it still hurts.'

Pam thinks, it was like being flayed, like having long strips of your skin torn away. Such hurt. You want to rub your eyes all the time, constantly. You want to erase it, crush it out of your brain, that picture that's outlined in black there, yes, there, right behind your forehead, branded into your consciousness: a picture of him doing the same things, saying the same things to someone else.

'Well now,' Madame Vilenska says, 'let me tell you about the Oblivion Treatment. This is the reason, incidentally, that all applicants for this position have to be so carefully interviewed. I have to find precisely the right staff, otherwise the Treatment might be jeopardized.'

'But what is it, this treatment?' Pam asks. Oblivion means forgetfulness . . . unconsciousness. She knows that.

'It is a skilful combination of hypnosis and certain very mild, non-addictive, oh, strictly non-addictive, substances.'

'Do you mean drugs?' Pam says. 'I'm having nothing to do with anything like that.'

Madame Vilenska says, 'No, no, child. Not drugs . . . goodness, no. Herbal infusions, tisanes, all strictly natural, growing things, nothing artificial at all.'

And how lucky, Madame Vilenska thinks, that no

one associates drugs with the scarlet tatters of the poppy, with the coca plant.

'But what does this treatment do? Is it a beauty treatment?' Pam asks.

'The Treatment eliminates unhappiness.'

'That's marvellous,' Pam says. 'But *can* you eliminate unhappiness?'

'Very easily.' Madame Vilenska nods.

Again, Pam is reminded of a lizard . . . such space between the eyes.

'You eliminate unhappiness,' Madame Vilenska continues, 'by eradicating memories.'

'Unhappy memories?'

'Yes, of course.'

'But what about the others?'

'The others? I don't understand you.' Madame Vilenska never permits herself to frown, but she inclines her head to the left, to indicate bewilderment.

'The happy memories . . .'

'I'm afraid they go also . . . along with all the rest. Along with the unhappy ones. Most people do not have such a treasury of happy memories that they are unwilling to . . . part with them.'

Pam says, 'Do people know? I mean . . . is it allowed . . . do your customers know that you do this? This Oblivion Treatment?'

'People?' Madame Vilenska smiles a little. Not too much. Smiling is nearly as hard on the face as frowning. 'Well, of course, my staff know. That is why I have to be so careful . . . so discreet . . . you understand, I'm sure. And one satisfied client passes the word to another, and so it goes . . . word of mouth. The most powerful form of advertising in the world.'

Pam is suddenly terrified: of Madam Vilenska, of the Salon, of the Treatment. She cannot, will not work here.

Pam says, 'I'm afraid I have to go now.'

Madame Vilenska says, 'But why? Can you not see that what I am doing is for the best? Can you not see that there are those who are longing, begging me to take away the unbearable weight of their memories?'

Pam says, 'Maybe that's true . . . but if you take *all* someone's memories away, you're turning her into a kind of . . . I don't know . . . a kind of zombie.'

'A zombie? Why? Why a zombie?'

'Because that's what a person is . . . really when you get down to it . . . a person *is* her memories. It's the memories, all of them, that make us all different. That make us who we are.'

'But it's memories that destroy us!' Madame Vilenska cries. 'I have blotted mine out totally. If it were not so, how could I have lived? After what I have seen . . .'

Madame Vilenska thinks, they are rubbed out. No longer there. As if I had taken the pictures and torn them across and across. Now they are tiny fragments, blown about in a strong wind . . . I catch a detail here and there. The rhythm of a train's wheels . . . the drifts of hair cut and cut and falling on the stone floor . . . smoke.

Pam says, 'That's all very well, but I want to remember everything. See it all, and feel it and remember it. Even if it hurts. I'm sorry.'

'I'm sorry too. You've led a very sheltered life. You would have made a good employee for Salon Vilenska. Never mind. I wish you every success in your career and I will press this buzzer and call in the next child.'

Pam thinks, why is she staring like that? I can't see anything except her eyes . . . they are darker and darker now and wider and wider apart and I want to take my eyes away from those eyes and look at something else, but I can't. That's all there is . . . and I'm drowning in them, falling and falling . . .

Pam says, 'Thank you very much, Madame Vilenska,' and walks towards the door. A skilful arrangement of mirrors shows Madame Vilenska scores of Pams on their way out: out and up and on to the rainy pavements of the real world. She presses her buzzer, looks down at the black filigree of lace stretching over her hands, and waits for the next applicant to sit down.

'You didn't get the job, then?' says Shirley.

'No. I was offered it, mind,' says Pam. 'At least, I think I was. But I didn't want it.'

'Why ever not? Posh salon like that. I think there's something wrong with you, I do, honestly. Some of us would give our eye teeth for a job like that.'

'It was weird. Madame Vilenska was weird.'

'Weird? How was she weird?'

Pam frowns. She says, 'I can't remember.'

# Whispers *from the* Hotel California

### *George*

It's amazing. After all this time, there are people out there still interested in what happened at the *Hotel California*. You, now. You must still have been in short trousers when we closed down. There were all sorts of rumours circulating about what went on there, even when we were the top night club in Manchester. We were big. Bigger than the *Hac*, or the *Ritz* or the *Banshee* or *Fifth Avenue* or any of the ones you've got now. I'm saying it as shouldn't, really, but I've never been one for false modesty. Still, *Hotel California* was my idea. My concept. My baby. Yes, I know the song came first. I know the song gave me the idea, but no one else thought of basing an entire nightclub around one song, did they? Just me.

When I suggested it, everyone thought I'd gone off my rocker. When I told them that it had to be 'Hotel California' and not 'Good Vibrations' or 'Strawberry Fields' or any other song that was around, they couldn't see it. 'Hotel California', I explained to them (and I had to be patient, they didn't get it at first), had a very strong image. We could model the whole place on the photograph that's on the album cover. And more than that, I said, have you ever listened to the words? They're sinister. Menacing. Dangerous. People love sinister things. Have you noticed? All is not what it seems in the Hotel California. There are voices in the corridor. There are steely knives, and there are two of the spookiest lines ever written, just to finish the whole thing off:

*You can check out any time you like,*
*but you can never leave.*

Those two lines give me a thrill every time I think about them. Well, I talked the money men round in the end. We got our Spanish-style baroque façade put up over an old Victorian warehouse . . . don't ask me where it was. It's gone now. Been bulldozed, which was probably the best thing for it. We put in corridors. We made the main dance area as much like the room on the album cover as we could: yellow light, arched windows set high up, a palm tree in the corner, hanging lamps imported from Mexico, and the bar set up to look like Reception in a hotel.

For weeks before we opened, we flyposted every wall we could. Black letters on yellow saying simply:

137

'Welcome to the *Hotel California*'. Black letters on blue saying: 'Plenty of room at the *Hotel California*', and black letters on pink saying: 'Living it up at the *Hotel California*'. We had flyers printed too, thousands of them. We blitzed the whole city with paper. You couldn't not know about us. Not if you lived in Manchester and looked about you.

For a while, it all worked. It was the place to be. Then came the death and after that, the police started nosing around, and started to connect up all sorts of other unexplained deaths. It seems the *Hotel California* had a high casualty rate, one way and another. People stopped coming after a while. You should speak to Reggie. He was the barman. He knew what went on. Better than me. I mean, I hardly ever went in there. Once a place is up and running, I kind of lose interest in it, know what I mean? It was just my concept. I liked the song so much, you see.

## Reggie

Yes, I was the barman at the *Hotel California*. They used to call me the Captain. It's in the words of the song, remember?

> *So I called up the Captain,*
> *please bring me my wine . . .*

I didn't mind. And it was Martha, I reckon, who was supposed to be the one with the Mercedes Benz, the one who drinks pink champagne on ice. And she

138

loved the song. She acted up to it, wandering around in her silver dress, sort of chanting, to anyone who would listen.

*We are all just prisoners here*
*of our own device . . .*

There was too much quoting altogether, if you ask me. I thought the whole idea was daft, if you want to know the truth. I mean, Manchester just isn't on a dark desert highway, whichever way you look at it. But George used to say, 'You leave image to me, Reggie, and get on with what you're good at – pulling pints.'

There wasn't much of that either. All these pink frothy drinks we used to have. Cocktails. Silly sweet stuff. Drinks for girls. I've not got anything against girls. You mustn't think that, but Martha and her crowd . . . they were different. I'd never seen girls like that before. For a start, they were a gang. They used to come in all together. They were all dressed the same, in shimmery silver dresses, like a kind of uniform. Martha was their leader. I often wonder what happened to them and to her. She was tall, with a white face and blonde hair that was nearly white too. Beautiful? I suppose so, in a bloodless sort of way. I suppose they all were, all the silver girls. Martha was the only one of them who ever spoke to me. Sometimes I thought she was the only one of them who ever spoke at all. Before the punters came in, she'd sit on a barstool and chat. Well, chat's not the right word, of course. She'd never just make a remark, you know, for the sake of being friendly. But she'd answer if you asked her things. A bit like squeezing blood out of a stone, as they say. I said once, 'Who're all your friends? Why do they all wear the same kind of clothes? Why don't they speak?' I still remember what she said.

She said, 'They're not my friends. They're my subjects. My troops in the battle.'

'Subjects?' I laughed. 'Fancy yourself as a queen, then?'

She didn't say anything at first, but she nodded at me. Then she said, 'Queen of the All-Night Dancing,' and showed her teeth. I won't call it a smile. It wasn't friendly enough to qualify as a smile.

'What's the All-Night Dancing?' I asked.

'It's a punishment,' she said. 'For certain kinds of men. You'll see.'

And I did see. I watched it going on every night for a year. Everyone danced at the *Hotel California*. It was a club, after all. But most people came and went. Stopped for a drink and a word or two with me. They came in couples. That was most people. The Silver Girls, though, were different. They never stopped. Whenever you looked at the floor, they were moving. And their partners . . . well, they were always young men on their own. The Silver Girls never let them rest. They never came up to the bar. They just danced. As the night went on, the young men would get weaker and weaker. Worn out, they were, by the time we closed. Martha never danced, though. Sometimes she watched from a barstool.

I said to her once, 'Got to hand it to those Silver Girls of yours. Got plenty of energy, haven't they?' and Martha smiled and quoted that dratted song again:

*Some dance to remember, some dance to forget.*

Well, that was how it was for a long time. Then one night, Glory came in, and things started to happen.

Glory's real name was Gloria, but her nickname suited her. She was dark and small and very pretty. She was mad for her boyfriend, Al. You could see that, a mile off. I always thought he was a bit too old for her, but I kept quiet. People are always telling me what an old stick-in-the-mud I am, and how old-fashioned and everything, so I didn't say anything, but I can remember thinking: he's been around and she hasn't. And the way she used to look at him made me shiver with a kind of dread of what would happen if he ever got fed up with her and left her for another woman, or something. He was dead smooth. All slicked-back hair and hundred quid shoes and rather too much gold jewellery. They made a handsome couple on the dance floor, I will say that. I suppose I realized, somewhere in my unconscious or something, that he was probably married. That sort of man often is. That's my experience. Glory's dream of love didn't last long. The night it happened is something I'd rather not talk about, if you don't mind. Jules was the bouncer at the time. He'll tell you what went on. I still have bad dreams about that night. Because Glory

. . . well, I felt that she was different. I felt she deserved better. Hit me hard. Very hard. It's still with me really, especially at night. There's a dream that I think of as a monster, lying in wait for me as I sleep. I can't rid myself of it. Like it says in the song:

> They stab it with their steely knives
> But they just can't kill the beast.

Look at that! You've got me quoting from it now. Go and talk to Jules. I try not to think about those days too much. Not if I can help it.

## Jules

Reggie sent you? Is that right? Blimey, I haven't heard from him in years. He OK? Good. Great. *Hotel California*, eh? Yeah, of course I remember what happened. I was the one who waited with Glory while the ambulance came. It was weird. I could have sworn . . . well, I'll tell it from the beginning, shall I? Right. Glory and Al came in early. They were dead lovey-dovey, anyone could see that. Reggie told you all about that, I bet. Right. Then after they've been in a couple of hours, and dancing so close that you'd swear they were welded together, this enormous stretch limousine turns up on the pavement outside. White. Smashing motor. I rush to open the door and say my lines. I have to say them to every customer. That's the rule.

142

*Plenty of room at the Hotel California,*
*any time of year, you can find it here.*

The woman who steps out of the car isn't even listening. She pushes right past me and goes barging in without paying, while I'm still stood there like a wally, hanging on to the limo door. I rush after her, to stop her, or get her to pay, or something, but by the time I've got to her, she's found Al. Well, I thought she was fancy stuff and Al was posh, but I've never heard a ding-dong battle like those two had that night. Everyone froze. The music stopped. It was like a boxing match or something. We were all . . . what's the word? . . . mesmerized, that's the word. We couldn't move. Anyway, the long and the short of it is: this fancy lady is none other than Al's lawful wedded missus, and he's being a naughty boy, bringing little Glory into the *Hotel California* behind Wifey's back. He swears blind there's nothing in it, they only come here to dance etc, etc, and I'm thinking, everyone's thinking: if she'll believe that, she'll believe anything. She doesn't believe it. She hauls Al off to the stretch limo and Glory's just left there, looking like a zombie. After Al and his missus leave, the music starts up again. We're all feeling a bit shaken, and the management want everyone dancing and feeling better as quickly as possible. Couples move on to the dance floor. We all look at Glory to see what she's going to do, and we heave a sigh of relief when we see she's dancing too. The relief doesn't last long, mind you. It's obvious, in a few minutes, that Glory's dancing is crazy. She's lost it. She's . . . I'm not good at describing stuff, but she's like blown around by the music. She's got no control. She's got her eyes staring, and the muscles round her mouth are twitching, and she's white, as white as all the Silver Girls and Martha, which is saying something. She dances over to the bar then, and grabs a glass before anyone can stop her, and twirls back to the middle of the dance floor. I didn't see what happened next, but I heard things. Seems Glory had crushed the glass in her bare hands and begun to slash at her wrists. They stopped her, of course, and Reggie phoned the ambulance. I sat next to her while we waited for it to come. She was white and her hands were red and her pretty dress was all dark with blood. She wasn't saying anything. Her eyes were closed. Lila has always said she was dead, but what I say is: how could she be dead? She was back in the *Hotel California* within days. I was gobsmacked, I can tell you, and not only because I thought I'd never see her again, but also because she'd joined the Silver Girls, seemed to be one of them. That was odd. I never could work it out. I didn't think I'd ever seen her talking to them. Just goes to show. No, I can't tell you about Al's death, although of course it was all over the papers. I'd left the *Hotel California* by then. Had enough. Like I say, the whole thing felt weird. Lila stayed to the end. She'd know more than most. She was a cocktail waitress or something. And she looked after the cloakroom. Did a bit of everything, did Lila. You go and talk to her.

I'm quite respectable now, aren't I? You'd never guess I'd been a cocktail waitress, would you? I tell you, I look at myself in the mirror lately and think: too many doughnuts, that's what's the matter with you! Anyway, you don't want to talk about me. It's what happened to Glory and Al, that's what you want to know, isn't it? Well, I know what I know, and the only reason I haven't told anyone before is because they'd lock me up. Barking mad, they'd say I was. Only I'm not. I know. How do I know? Because I saw what I saw and also because Martha told me. She told me later.

The thing is, Glory died the night she slashed her wrists. I was there and I saw it. All that blood. I know she came back to the *Hotel California*. It makes no difference. She was dead. Yes, I suppose I'm saying she was a ghost or a zombie or something, and no, I don't do drugs and I never drink either. That's not everything. They all were. All the Silver Girls. And Martha. Queen of the All-Night Dancing, she called herself. Dead, every single one of them. She told me straight out, Martha did. We were in the Ladies together. She was just standing there, by the long mirror.

'Why do you call yourself that?' I asked. 'Queen of the All-Night Dancing?'

'Because that's what Eternity is for me,' she answered. 'And for the Silver Girls. A dance. Going on and on.'

I thought she was being hippy-ish. She was forever quoting from that song. She loved it. Once she said, 'It's about Death, you know. All that stuff about Heaven and Hell, and the voices in the corridor welcoming you. Just one huge hotel waiting for the dead to check in. That's what I think it is.'

I didn't answer because I was fixing my lipstick at the time, but I was thinking that the words didn't necessarily mean that. It depended how you looked at it . . . anyway, where was I? Oh, right, all the Silver Girls were zombies. That was what Martha was telling me. So I wasn't surprised to see Glory. More sad, really. Martha liked telling me things. Once she said, 'Anyone we dance with doesn't last long.'

'Why?' I said. 'What happens to them?'

'Oh,' said Martha. 'They grow very weak. They just fade away.'

That was what happened to Al. He came back to find Glory. He thought she was alive, of course. Most people did. We never thought Al would have the courage to come back to the *Hotel California* after that scene with his wife. But he did. Then I saw that he really loved Glory. If she'd been alive, everything would have been fine. They'd have run away together or something. All right, I know it's cloud-cuckoo land, but it does happen sometimes and it would have with those two. I know it would. As things stood, Glory was . . . I don't know how to put it . . . pre-programmed. Now that she'd become a Silver Girl, she had to do what all the Silver Girls did, and dance her partner to death. It was a bit unfortunate that Al died right there on the dance floor. By the time the police arrived, she was gone. I've never seen her again. All the Silver Girls and Martha simply vanished. Oh, I know there was a crowd there that night and everyone was milling around the body, but someone ought to have seen a whole line of pale women in silver dresses leaving the place, don't you think? No one did. Or no one ever *said* they did. Later on, the police found out that a lot of unexplained deaths (healthy young men dancing in a club one night and dead in their beds the next) sort of led back to the *Hotel California*. They talked to everyone. We told them about Martha and the Silver Girls. We all described them. There were more witnesses saying they'd seen Glory dancing with Al just before he died than you've had hot dinners. They searched for her. No one knew where she came from. Reggie the barman had a fuzzy picture of her taken the previous Christmas and they used that in the papers . . . enlarged it and everything, but no one seemed to know her. For a bit, all the kerfuffle made the *Hotel California* dead popular, but stories started going round. A rival club put out leaflets with the last lines of the song printed on them. White on black, I remember.

> *Last thing I remember, I was*
> *running for the door.*
> *I had to find the passage back*
> *to the place I was before.*
> *'Relax,' said the Night Man.*
> *'We are programmed to receive.*

*You can check out any time you like*
*but you can never leave.'*

Those words send shivers up my spine to this very day. The song spooks me. I love it and it spooks me. I sing it a lot.

Anyway, business dropped off so much, they had to close. The place stood empty for ages and then it was bulldozed. My brother went past there one night when it was all boarded-up. He had a look in through the planks, and swears to this day he heard music playing and a yellowish light shining, but I reckon he was most probably drunk. Don't you think that's the most likely explanation? It's either that, or Martha and the Silver Girls were back there, doing their All-Night Dancing. Take your pick.